# THE ORIGINS OF A STAR

C. McEntee

SUBJUNCTIVE
*an Imperative Press imprint*

Hampden, ME

Published by Subjunctive
An Imprint of Imperative Press Books
Hampden, Maine
Imperativepressbooks.com/imprints

Publisher's Note: This is a work of fiction. Names, characters, places, and incidents are a product of the author's imagination. Locales and public names are sometimes used for atmospheric purposes. Any resemblance to actual people, living or dead, or to businesses, companies, events, institutions, or locales is completely coincidental.

Book Layout © 2017 BookDesignTemplates.com

**The Origins of a Star/ C. McEntee** -- 1st ed.
ISBN 978-1-957451-00-8

Horror | Horror – Psychological | Horror – Occult and Supernatural
Fantasy | Fantasy – Dark Fantasy

Cover design by Urquhart Illustrations, A.E. Urquhart

To my family

# CONTENTS

# Creation

*400 years ago, in a distant universe*

"Madam Corsseussula! How wonderful to make your acquaintance once again, my lady!"

The heavenly voice spilt the peaceful atmosphere ringing out with a painfully obnoxious amount of cheer. A young man with a braid that consisted solely of pure white strands of hair, like candy floss hanging down his back that swayed as he walked, exclaimed the words like a child on Christmas day, cheerfully gliding toward the tall woman with a cloak that floated around her figure like an astral mass of stars. She contrasted his appearance greatly, but was in no way any less elegant or beautiful. Her eyes, which she had four of, had no irises or pupils, gleaming a color of simply pure white, like swirling heavenly portals embedded in her polished flesh. Her hair was the same, although as one shifted on their feet, her locks became somewhat iridescent and glowing, and floated like liquid on her scalp, cascading down her back as smooth as a waterfall. To say she was tall was a massive under-statement. The goddess was towering, and she had to crane her neck to glimpse the speaker, who was about as tall as her calf. Her skin was a shimmery indigo, and she wore a crest of a beautiful stone, an opal, held up by glimmering silver on her head, almost resembling a crown, although she detested it when it was called such a thing. The cloak she wore hovered ever so faintly around her form, with ever-changing hues of light and dark making up the odd fabric – or was it even fabric?

Her lips were full and plump and slightly parted as she turned to meet the newcomer. They were a shade of beautiful dark blue that made them pop out even more. She was stunningly beautiful, almost impossibly gorgeous, and it was obvious she knew her worth by her attitude.

Even the strongest mortal male would tremble under such a gaze, such a glare. It was just how the star goddess was, even if she was completely calm. She could make every being in every reality weak at the knees with just a stare, just a mere glance in their direction. She was simply so intimidating, so graceful…so much, in fact, that even looking in her direction would make anyone feel trivial. Trivial and insignificant compared to such a strong and magnificent woman.

The snowy-haired male could not have differed more from the regal lady in blue before him. His skin had a slight pallor to it, as pale the moonlight itself, and shone in the presence of the goddess, like light bouncing off of rolling tides in the ocean. His flesh nearly seemed to glisten, as if he'd been showered with a light film of dew, and his form was decently muscular, as the defined muscles in his arms could be easily seen through the cloth he wore. He was clad in soft white silks, wrapped carefully around his strong figure, decorated with calla lilies near his chest and his neck, and larkspurs woven into his hair, purple peeking out through snow. The airy silks were a light bark shade and a few delicate strings held up the front. He wore no shoes at all, and atop his head of pure bone-white hair, in addition to the violet larkspurs, were two horns resembling a deer's. They were towering and solid, and strung between them were petite and narrow vines of washed-out flowers and other plants. Moss clung to the base of them, not unlike how it would typically attach to the roots of trees. Judging solely by the look Corsseussula gave the odd features on his head, she found them to be a waste of space.

His facial features were round and plump with youth, not a blemish on his finely crafted, milky white skin. His blue eyes shone with a sense of joy, the pale azure irises glowing softly. The epitome of perfection, the definition of what any human would envision to be a personified version of the very Earth itself.

Both ethereal beings stood inside of a clear space where no reflections were shown. It was simply…empty. There was no surrounding land, no water, no trees, no dirt, no buildings, no far-off towns with cozy fireplaces sending puffs of smoke out of lively chimneys, no overgrown gardens full of bursting harvest. No air. No sound. It was as if everything and nothing had collided in a beautiful explosion of 'in between.' It was tranquil and still, which is what the Star Goddess admired deeply. It must have been why she was there.

Of course, perhaps it was also the reason why she bristled so much at hearing such an irritatingly joyful voice yell out her name.

Corsseussula glared down at the man below her as if he were an ugly blot on a perfect piece of white robes.

"Hold," she uttered and held up her hand, her voice echoing. The man obeyed her and stopped, grinning affectionately despite her expression of utter loathing. Either he chose to ignore such a stare, or he hadn't noticed.

"It has been far too long, hasn't it, my lady?"

She narrowed her eyes at him and lifted her hand once more to wave him off, unimpressed. For her, apparently it hadn't been long enough.

"It has been merely a millennium, Aethis. You have spent a far longer time daydreaming."

She turned to face away from him after speaking and stood still, waiting for Aethis to leave. After hearing no footsteps and whirling back around to find him still staring up at her with his annoyingly perfect sky-blue eyes, she was not thrilled in the slightest. Her lip curled in outright disgust at the sheer audacity of the god below her, the darkness on her face rivaling that of a madman.

"You know well you are not welcome here. I am done with your persistence, your asks of me. I am sick of it! I

have done enough! What is it you want from me now?"
she demanded, her tone seeming to drip with absolute
disdain. How dare he ask another favor of her? And she
knew well that was what he came here to do, she was no
ignorant fool. His little 'happy reunion' attempt was pathetic. And she knew the god before her knew so as well,
so why had he even bothered? Aethis folded his hands
together politely and put on a soft smile.

"Don't be quite so harsh, my lady. I come with no will
to harm."

"No will to harm?! No will to harm?!" she boomed,
face turning from calm yet annoyed to frustrated and in-
sulted. She pointed to Aethis.

"You are Death's creator, Death's friend, Aethis. All
you bring is punishment and woe. Spare me the lies and
deceit."

Aethis put on a look of pleading at her words and
looked up at her. She showed no sympathy.

"Creating something does not quite mean that one is
fond of—"

"Spare me."

Aethis almost pouted at her immediate shutdown of his
attempt at a peaceful protest, and he swiftly let out a large
overdone exhale of despair, clutching his pale hands to his
bandaged chest in glorified agony. Corsseussula had to
press her lips together to smother any words that might
have escaped her lips about how his act reminded her of a
distressed widow.

"Oh, but my lady, I require your assistance!" he responded, sadly lowering his head with downturned pink lips. "You see, my beautiful, delicate puppets are suffering, ever so! I have tried every method ever created to bring my wonderful friends to life, but they cannot live! Their hearts refuse to beat and their lungs expel any breath I give them! Though I have given them the truest bodies and minds, they do not breathe, nor do their hearts beat with life! It's simply astounding!"

Corsseussula frowned at his words, as if his whole rant were something she had heard several times before. She didn't like Aethis in general, finding him overly childish and persistent, and she hated how he used his words and bonds to other gods and goddesses, and had never in history agreed on any form of deal with him before. But for him to be asking that kind of request from her out of the blue with no genuine reason made her even more reluctant than she already was…

"'Tis of no concern to me whether your little toys can breathe and live. There are plenty of things in this vast universe that don't live and nobody ever complains. That's simply what puppets are meant for, no? Come now, Aethis, I at least thought you had some intelligence, some common sense, or some humility at the least, but you have ultimately proven me wrong with just a few words. In response to your request, my answer is no. I have no interest in this," she told him, lifting her chin as she addressed the situation.

He gave her a pitiful smile, almost begging her to simply feel a hint of sympathy. Considering Corsseussula, though, the chances of that happening were completely impossible. So he pushed farther with his request, adding in a few other excuses. "Madam Corsseussula, you assisted Laphanae in the creation of humanity. I wish to—"

She slammed her foot down on the crystal floors of her realm the moment she heard Laphanae's name. "Silence!"

Her voice echoed, and the clear realm turned from pure and spotless to a swirling mess of space masses and clusters of uneven time. Her anger radiated from everywhere. Anyone, sane or insane, rich or poor, god or human, would have trembled at the Star Mistress's fury. But Aethis just stood, face one of pure amazement at her demeanor change from just a name he dared to speak.

"I will not allow such a fool of a deity as yourself to wreak havoc with…with puppets using my ability! How dare you even—"

"Oh, Madam Corsseussula, how radiant you glow…how bright a rage you have…" Aethis praised her with eagerness. It was like he was almost…excited at her fury. Eager to see more. Begging to see more.

"Silence!" she shouted. "You have no right to demand anything of me, you lowly figure! I've had enough of you! Enough of your flavorless attempts at sweetening whatever horrid 'agreement' you wish to strike with me! I've rejected every deal and have only been reluctant with favors! I have reached my limit with you! I am done! That is it!"

Aethis only nodded, still smiling brightly. "Of course, Star Mistress. You're absolutely correct. I apologize for my rude demand."

Corsseussula paused, unsure she heard him correctly.

"…What?" she asked, voice a tad quieter, but still sharp. She was still plenty angry, but now she was astounded. Aethis gave an apologetic bow.

"I'm apologizing. I said you are quite correct, Star Mistress. How foolish of me to assume you'd drop everything for my request."

He turned away. She stood there, shocked, but still aware of herself. She was a figure of grace and mystery and must act as such. Besides, Aethis not arguing further was such a rare thing. Better savor it while she could. She stood up straight and nodded.

"Well then."

Aethis nodded as well, walking away. A sharp-toothed grin slowly spread on his lips before he spoke up softly.

"Of course, I'm sure you are well aware of the price it comes with. I've been plenty lenient…but perhaps it's about time I told Laphanae about what truly happened to his mother."

She whipped around to look back at him, the calm aura vanishing as quickly as he spoke those last three words. Her expression was unreadable, but her mind was working at the very speed of light. How dare he, a lower god of creation, threaten her, the very creator of the universes and space that made up all of time and existence itself!

How dare he bring up that horrid woman she'd accidentally killed in a fit of rage all those many years ago?! It's not like it was even her fault! She was meant to kill her. Why else would the woman fall so easily?

Although those thoughts ran through her divine head confidently, her voice still carried an edge of fear.

"You wouldn't dare, Aethis. Surely you're not that much of a fool that you would—"

"A shame, truly."

His eyes were boring into her, and he smiled widened. He repeated himself slowly, making himself appear all the more unsettling. Corsseussula simply looked at him, her expression hardening as she realized she'd been backed into a corner.

"I—"

"Such. A. Shame."

She closed her mouth and knelt down to look him dead in the eye. He had her, and he knew it. She couldn't let word get out that she'd killed Laphanae's mother. It would break Laphanae's heart, even if he knew his mother was comparable to a leech. Bastard Aethis with his threats. She never should have called for his assistance in getting rid of that woman. Now, her face was expressionless, but there was a look in her eyes. A look of both fear and hardened anger. But also a look of authority. She was still certain of herself, even though she was clearly going to have to agree to the terms of this twisted cooperation.

"Listen to me, Aethis. I'll play along with this pointless, horrible deal. I will infuse the life of starlight into each of your puppets, shape the stars into their souls. They will live."

Aethis smiled widely and clapped his hands together like a small child. "It's very nice when people cooperate," he remarked cheerfully. "Very good, madam. We'll start right away then."

Her expression didn't change. She leaned closer to Aethis, her face one of loathing, but also lined with the knowledge and cunning of millennia worth of logic and psychology and common sense. Her voice was low, in warning.

"Aethis, do you know what I am?"

"A horrible wife."

She had to hold back a thousand retorts to his effortless mockery of her, all while he stood with that ear-to-ear smirk of his. She inhaled deeply, her mighty chest rumbling as her lungs filled, and she continued on as if no answer had been given to her.

"I am the Mother of Stars, Aethis. If you put my starlight into those puppets, that makes them my children."

"I created them though, madam. Truly, that makes them my children."

She stared him in the eyes, and a tiny smile curled the sides of her mouth.

"All the same, a piece of me in their souls makes me their creator. So if you hurt my children, use them for anything other than what you claim to do — just an "experiment" of sorts — and they look to the stars above for help, I'm going to come down there and throttle you."

~

To gods, years pass like seconds. Blink, and two years have soared by. Fall asleep for an evening, and seven hundred of them pass. Although time passed quickly for them, creating Aethis' little puppets was a difficult and drawn-out task. Giving life to something was no easy feat, after all.

Finally, centuries after the decision had been made, the puppets were successfully created. Corsseussula had done as she promised, although with much resistance and harsh obscenities muttered under bated breath. Soon, all of these odd star-born creatures were created. Well, almost all of them.

Corsseussula knelt down graciously in the field realm where Aethis dwelt. Unlike her chamber of solitude, simply clear and empty, this realm was full, as full as it could be. It was a lovely place, lush with endless greenery and flowers. It was arranged simply. Surrounding her, there were a few bushes of flowers, then a beautifully serene lake slightly off in the distance, shaded by a slouching willow tree, its droopy branches kissing the soft waters of the lake every time a gentle wind caressed their leaves. The sky was dusk, swirling with lavender and pale blue and a few flecks of pink and white occasionally sprinkled in, like afterthoughts of the atmosphere. The blades of grass bent over under her weight were a healthy green, and all the other grass patches swayed ever so slightly with the breeze. All of this was enjoyable on its own, but the flowers were what made it seem unique. Each one was a gorgeous bloom, a flower that began in lavender at the tips of its opening petals, like grand welcome carpets, with the color slowly fading into white. They were definitely something to appreciate, with reaching petals and sweet scents, but the star goddess paid none of them any mind. She had seen hundreds of the same ones before.

She reached over and took a small doll-like figure. She examined it, tracing her finger over the dips and cracks on its face.

"What's this one's name?" she asked Aethis, who stood beside her, for once, a solemn look on his face as he watched her work. Around and behind him were dozens more puppets. Piles of drooping dolls, stacked on top of each other, tossed here, placed there, some with long hair, some with short, some with none. All of the puppets were scattered at and under his feet.

Only, they weren't just puppets anymore, no.

They were all unconscious, eyes closed and bodies limp. Each one's chest rose and fell with breath, and each one had a heart inside that throbbed like any other human's. The only real distinct differences from humans were their wider eyes, oddly perfect skin, and some of them had more vibrant hair.

But they were alive.

"I haven't bothered to name him. He's just a puppet after all."

The goddess sighed in annoyance and stood up, still holding the puppet. She tilted her head to the sky and reached up.

A delicate, glistening stream of light, like an airy form of water, cascaded down from a nearby star perched in the heavens and flowed like honey into her hand. She closed her palm, took the starlight carefully, and pressed her palm against the tiny puppet boy's forehead. A tiny diamond mark was imprinted smoothly on the skin of his forehead for a moment and flashed brightly–just once–before retreating into the pale pink of his skin, disappearing. Corsseussula paused for a moment and then shifted her hand through a loose part of her long and flowy robe and pulled out a thin strand of pure sunlight with shifting orange, yellow, and red hues. She wrapped it around the puppet's wrists. It immediately almost seemed to turn into skin and flesh, settling like it was always a part of his body.

"What's that for, Star Mistress?" Aethis asked, leaning to peek over her shoulder. She gave him a glare and then looked back at the puppet in her hands, whose skin now grew warm and soft. He let out a small hum before turning over, remaining asleep like the others. She handed the puppet to Aethis reluctantly.

"Well, that was a remnant of the first sunset to ever happen on the surface of Earth itself. My dearest gifted it to me."

"Really? Whyever would you waste something as precious as that on my puppet?!"

She gave him a sharp look, almost like an annoyed mother who's sick of dealing with a no-good son.

"His name is not 'puppet'. I shall name him…"

"Fine. If you truly wish to, I suggest something easy. Yureni. After the sunset."

"…right. Fine. As for the 'wasteful use'…I gave it to him as a gift. Since he has arisen from the stars, he is now my son, no? And so I am entitled to protect him. Like the others."

"I doubt your 'son' is worth anything more than a toy for me to test out."

"You'll see."

Though many gods are often cunning, and deceitful, there is always a common rule most seemed to follow. Gods and goddesses of any and every realm are always very devoted to promises. If they truly promise something, they would never break it. And Corsseussula had no intention of lying to Aethis about protecting her strange 'children.'

Eventually, Aethis created a world to keep his puppets in, and, day in and day out, he would observe them. But he grew frustrated. Nothing exciting was happening. Sure, nothing bad was happening, but everything was just boring. He'd made these puppets based after humans and the Earth. So why on Earth were they refusing to act like humanity?

Aethis would often rant to the goddess of stars about this, who truly didn't care if he was upset.

He stood in his realm alongside her, critiquing both his puppets and humans. "Humanity truly is pathetic." he said bitterly, kneeling in his meadow of pale, sickly blossoms. He lifted a hand with a lavender-hued flower to his face, inches away from his chin.

"Humans and puppets alike think they're so smart."

He chuckled to himself, though it held no true joy, twirling the flower almost thoughtfully. His tone was light and playful, but there was sharpness that bit at the edge of his voice.

"Thinking they've solved a problem when they've really just created another that will cause them to crash and burn once again. Refusing to do anything interesting at all. Living like livestock"

He tipped his head back and laughed, his voice echoing in the soundless world. He returned his gaze to the small bloom in his hand.

"Thinking they're higher than me." He spat the last part, and the blossom began to leak a deep red, smearing his hand.

Corsseussula stood beside him, staring intently ahead of her, not at her company. She paid no mind to his frustration, but she pondered his words for a moment.

"You're the superior being in your mind, Aethis?"

Aethis was still. Then he crushed the flower in his hand and let out a soft giggle, almost mockingly.

"Oh, dear, sweet friend," He said lightly and softly, with a note of hysterics in his voice. He looked back at her, dead in the eyes, and smiled a bit.

"I am far superior to any other god there is out there. Even more than you."

Silence.

Aethis' smile subsided, curling into something similar to an annoyed frown at her lack of response. He rose and strode away from the tall woman, and, as he did, the faint bluish glows from the flowers around him began to wink out one by one. The woman did not move her gaze away from Aethis, all four pale eyes simply watching as he walked away. She paused for a brief moment, and when he was almost out of earshot, she called out,

"You're wrong."

Aethis stopped where he was and turned, an eyebrow raised in curiosity at her statement. His look was not unlike an excited predator's before catching their prey. He said nothing in response, and waited for her to elaborate. Corsseussula lifted her chin, expressionless.

"A devil is the lowest possible thing one could be."

Aethis gave her a wolf-like grin as the last, delicate flower's pale light snapped off, and the child of sunset and star, bound in chains, opened his eyes.

# The Beginning

The young child awakens. Or perhaps the old man.

Or maybe he isn't anything more than someone's whisper of an idea. Well, any of these statements may be true. This peculiar young man isn't sure himself.

Oh, heavens above, the poor thing. So new and naive, he doesn't even know his own name. Like a newborn, he sits up reaching for the sky. For the world. He lies in a large patch of perfectly green grass, and the light swallows up his face.

He is like an angel. Oh, how beautiful. So pure.

But that horrified look on that lovely face makes it ever so hard to see any form of perfection. Pesky thing. He should be happy. He is in a gorgeous place, in lavish white silks…

Oh, right. The little creature is disoriented.

The young man whips his head around, to and fro, like a crazed man, as if searching for something long gone. He presses his long fingers to his temples, his breath heaving in his chest as though he had just awoken from some terrible fright. His fingers run through his pale hair anxiously.

Breathe. Stroke. Breathe. His expression of distress does never once fade from his darling features. He swallows hard, Adam's apple bobbing in his throat as he glances around, searching for just a fraction of familiarity.

All around him, there is life at its peak. There are plants in the grass emitting a warm and soft glow, trees with long, flowing trails of silken leaves that shift as the fading aura of daylight prevails, and the stone ruin next to him is bathed in orange light that is shifting to a dark red. The stone ruin itself is a magnificent thing, such a granular chunk of rock, a monument, almost, even if it is weathered and crumbling. Once, perhaps, some kind of temple marking or a statue of worship. Perhaps even the gravestone of some unsung hero, forgotten over the millennia.

Vines snake up the broken pillar adorned with a few white rocks layered around the base, like a foundation for a mighty building, perhaps even a temple.

He looks around to try and find any signs of other intelligent life, but he sees none. Only the quiet nature surrounding his form. It is frighteningly perfect, horribly peaceful, agonizingly right. He stops his quick sightseeing and goes to lift himself from the ground. He notices very quickly as he rises that the hands that push him away from the earth do not fit with his body. They do not fit on his body at all. Those nimble fingers and skin that seems to shimmer in the light cannot be his. His hands are not like that. His hands…well…they're…. What are they?

What do they look like?

The young man stares at his hands as if he is staring at the face of a complete stranger. He cannot remember what his hands look like. Though perhaps he never bothered to look. That must be it. It's exactly like him to be ignorant about such small things.

Or is it?

The young man cannot remember.

He cannot even remember who he is. If he is even alive. Perhaps he is dead. Perhaps he isn't. He cannot remember anyone who would care either way. This, of course, sends the young man into a bit of a panic.

Who am I?

Such a ridiculous question.

Names are funny things. Labels to identify each other with is all they really are.

Without a name, is he considered unidentified? Without a name, does he have any meaning?

*Is he truly even real?*

Of course, he is real. He has to be, right? If he is thinking, isn't he real? If he has thoughts, doesn't that make him real? Don't real people have thoughts? All of a sudden, the young man is not so sure. He can breathe, and he feels a slight tip-tip throbbing in his neck, so he has a heartbeat. But he has no memories. That can't be right. Only infants have such a lack of something as crucial as memories, and so, he must have them.

…at least, he has a feeling he did.

Oh well. Thinking about this makes his head hurt. He looks up to observe further surroundings. Perhaps the position of the sun will tell him what time it is.

The sky is a sunset, he can see. It is dark, and yet he can see every detail of the tree with silver leaves only a few feet away from him. Around the edges of the grassy meadow, he can see a thick wad of clouds —mist— with a silvery orange hue to it, reflecting the apricot sky above. It shrouds the land beyond what he can see, seeming more like a brick wall rather than simple mist or fog. Why? Because, for some strange reason, the fog is impossible to see through. It's more like…a white blanket draped over the corners of this unfamiliar place.

He is quite close to a small portion of this odd fog. Curiosity strikes him suddenly. It's as if a small child is observing the world. What…what is this? He waits for a good moment and then sticks out a curious hand with reaching fingertips, trying to feel through it, trying to get a sense of what exactly it is. A sharp, burning sensation shoots through his arm and he recoils, forced to pull away. He winces in pain and rubs his hand. And a sound slips out from his lips.

"Ow."

The first word he has spoken.

But he has spoken before, hasn't he? This darling boy must have. Yet the words come fresh and new. Like something refreshing, something different.

The portion of fog where his hand had been swirls slightly, and he can see a faint outline of something through it. Someone, maybe? He simply cannot tell.

The fog settles almost as quickly as it had been disturbed, and a hush surrounds him on all sides. Not even the wind dares to make a single sound. He turns back to face the ground where he had woken up.

Well, not really woken up. But more of…arrived? Why is that the first thing that he thinks of? He dismisses the thought with a quick frown. Near where he is standing, a bit to the left of his foot, pale and bare, is a crystal pool of clear water around the size of three large tree stumps in a singular row and shaped like a bubble in the lush earth. The water has an orange-colored hue from the sky above, and it could be described as interesting how the cool water seems to sync with the sky. Mirror images, truly. He leans down next to the shallow pool. He is quite fascinated by such a beautiful reflection. While observing the sky within the reflection, eventually, his eyes come 'round to meet another pair of irises in the water. He nearly jumps before realizing the water mirrors this as well, and he is simply staring back at a face belonging to him.

As he stares at what appears to be his reflection, he sees nothing but someone else who mirrors his movements perfectly. His hair is white, but not with age, as the rest of him looks quite young, and it cascades down his back in soft layers. His face is youthful and healthy, along with the rest of his figure. His skin is entirely olive-colored. Not even a flush on his cheeks, a shadow of a wrinkle on his brow. His eyes are a dark gray, and they have pupils blown wide. He is clothed in a silky white top and white pants with a hue of yellow, making them a warm vanilla color, almost like buttercream.

*I am not myself.*

That much is true, he knows. How could he not know? The figure he sees in the water is most certainly not himself. He does not or, more did not, have pure white hair, that's simple logic. Humans, people, everyone he has ever met, do not have such a feature. Perhaps albino hair, but not one of such pure empty color.

White hair is most definitely not something he can remember having. Then again, he can't remember much at all. About himself, mostly. How he appeared to others and himself before, how he felt. His hobbies, his interests, his dislikes…it's like everything defining him has gone, all that's left are just random memories, as if someone had taken his mind and sewn it like a mismatched patterned quilt. Maybe pure white hair is normal and he is simply disoriented and confused?

*What a pity. Such a doll. Must be The Aurum.*

What? The thought floats to the top of his head, but it is not his own. He is then hit with a wave of confusion. Not his? What the hell?

Aurum. That word…he ponders it for a moment. The Aurum? He's never once heard of such a phrase. He pauses briefly before his eyes light up a bit. Perhaps it is his name.

So it must be. He must be called Aurum. With this newfound information, he decides that maybe he could try to introduce himself to surrounding people, if he can find any, and hope that they may know him or of people who will.

Aurum is about to leave, to try and find someone to question or somewhere to go, when he realizes the reflection that once followed his own movements, has changed. It is now someone else. Another young man with a full head of off-white, almost cream-colored hair, one of his messy bangs a muted red, as if his hair had somehow rusted. His hair flows just a bit below his ears, almost like the water itself, and he looks at Aurum with a solemn expression, as if indifferent about seeing him there, the complete opposite of Aurum's own expression. Aurum is far beyond what would be considered puzzled. More like bewildered. In shock?

Well, something along those lines. Why is there someone else there?

Perhaps he is dreaming. This must be some kind of symbolism. Perhaps this is a sign to him. He must consult someone about this once he wakes up.

He realizes quickly that this reflection is not his own— or rather, the body he saw before that he apparently possesses for now—but another. The man in the water puts a hand on the edge of the surface and mouths something, breathless. He repeats his silent sentence, eyes growing with a strange sense of urgency, as if trying to warn Aurum of something. But what? He doesn't look affected by the water at all, so why is he trying to talk to Aurum? What is even going on?

He reaches out to try and ripple the water, thinking it's an illusion or perhaps his reflection after all. Maybe if Aurum moves the water around, this odd man will disappear. Disappear and leave Aurum the hell alone, because he doesn't need all of this all at once.

Maybe it truly is some kind of reflection? After all, Aurum doesn't seem to be himself anymore.

But something tells him that may be a stretch of his disorientation. As he reaches into the water, rippling the surface of the cool, glassy puddle, the reflection in it surprisingly reaches out as well. He reaches with thin, pale fingers and grabs Aurum's hand. Aurum notices for the first time that this man's wrists are bound.

Bound with chains.

They look to be made of some kind of metal, perhaps silver or some kind of rock. They look to be tightly cuffed onto his pale wrists, the skin around them an angry red and irritated with dried blood that had crusted to a burgundy color. He yanks Aurum's hand all of a sudden, as if he's playing tug-of-war with his fingers, those pale hands clinging to him, turning white and veiny with strain.

Strain? It's just water…

It takes maybe a minute or so before he manages to get a good and firm grip on Aurum's wrist, and in that moment he pulls himself up out of the water.

Well, not exactly. But he manages to break his head free from the water and stares up at Aurum breathing hard. Aurum backs away in surprise at the figure and tries to let go of its hand, but it's already grabbing onto his forearm like it's his lifeline, taking deep and shaky breaths, coughing to clear its lungs of any water trapped within them.

Aurum is able to get a better look at the man. The silvery water from the pool has left his hair damp and dripping, and water drips onto his nose. He is wearing a pure white cloak that swirls around his still submerged torso, like a cloud of silk in the water, almost. He looks rather pale in the face too, not just the hands, and his breath comes out in sharp gasps as the color slowly returns to his cheeks.

Aurum gives him a moment to catch his breath, as he seems to be panting hard. This makes sense, as he had appeared to be fully submerged in water only seconds before. Aurum wonders how long he has been underwater. Apparently a long time, since his breath is heaving in his chest. He looks up at Aurum with his storm-cloud-gray eyes as his breathing slows to a regular speed. His eyes are not wide anymore. They are soft and kind, and a little relieved. As if the other had just saved his life, or rescued a family member of his. But he only pulled him out of the water. Partially, too. The man's head is out of water, that is all. He inhales and speaks with a soft and gentle voice. It has a slight rasp, as if he hasn't used it properly for dozens of years.

"Thank you."

He smiles as he says this, and grasps onto his cloak, still sopping wet. He looks eternally grateful, even if Aurum hasn't exactly done anything. Perhaps the man just wanted some acknowledgement. Sad.

Oh well.

Aurum wants to smile back honestly, even just out of pity because the man below him looks and sounds like some sort of madman, but something stops him. This doesn't feel right. Aurum doesn't know why, but something seems strange. The way the breeze felt earlier is different now. This man's grip feels different, his stare, the ground, the sky, the world...

Aurum can't place what exactly it is, but something is definitely not how it should be.

The man pauses before biting his lip as he looks toward the sky. And then he freezes and his grip on Aurum's wrist tightens significantly, almost cutting off his circulation. Aurum yelps and instinctively tries to break away from the other's iron grip yet again, but the man stops him. Aurum doesn't know why he's acting this way, who he is, why he's there, or what he saw, but now, Aurum doesn't exactly have much concern left, he just wishes this man would let go of his arm before he tears it off.

The cold metal from the man's chains is pressing down firmly onto Aurum's forearms, and as he glances back at him, they dig further into flesh. Aurum notices his eyes are filled with a new emotion. Several, in fact.

Sympathy. Uncertainty. Fear. And a bit of realization.

Aurum doesn't really like the way he's looking at him. The odd man senses his unease and sighs.

"Goddammit," he mumbles plainly before lifting his other hand above the water, with less of a struggle than the first one, surprisingly enough.

"Look, listen, m'really sorry for this—"

Aurum doesn't even have time to respond before the man grabs his arm with both hands, pulling him into the water with a harsh tug. And then Aurum cannot see anymore. He tries to reach out to the air, to grab onto something, but he only feels emptiness. And then a feeling of dread settles in the pit of his stomach as he hears a splash from above and feels cool metal press up on the flesh of both his wrists. Shortly after, Aurum feels himself being dragged lower, slowly, but surely.

He falls and falls. Does it ever end? Will he ever be the same again? He simply closes his eyes and lets the darkness of the water overcome him.

# The Man and the Child

"I serve no purpose to this world."

The small girl next to the man draped in a pale cloak stopped her humming to look at him. Her blonde hair, gathered up in a small braid that only reached around her shoulders, swayed lightly as the warm breeze from above caressed their faces. She tilted her head in curiosity and confusion. She did not understand. Perhaps she never would. He almost pitied her. He knew how she felt. Deprived of any and all knowledge of the world simply due to her age. Being told countless times 'You'll understand once you are older,' and 'I'll explain once you are old enough to explain it to me instead.' In his opinion, the children should be told these things. Being exposed to things like these at young ages means you have more time to think, to consider. To fully understand.

If a man spends all of life simply searching for an answer, he ends up wasting it and dies unsatisfied. It is better for the man to know and be upset for a bit then to live in fear and uncertainty his whole life with the 'what if' questions scattering across his brain like marbles.

"What do you mean?"

She asked, frowning. Her tone was one of partial curiosity, as if she could already predict what he was going to say. How he hated it when she gave him that look, her eyes staring up at him, wide with interest, vibrant irises glistening in the pale light sifted through the leaves of the swaying trees. Because of that very glance, this little young lady knew about every single angle of his mind, every section of his essence, every portion of his feelings. She could take his soul with simply one look. He didn't have the heart to lie to such a child as she, how could he ever? That little girl tore into his soul with her gaze, and she knew it.

"Hemera…I don't have any true meanin' here, do I? I must be crazy. Aren't I?" he asked her softly as he stared out at the horizon. Of course, it wasn't a real question that required a real answer. He already knew the answer well, and yet he was still not quite ready to fully accept the whole fact. The child beside him was aware of this and remained silent. He continued, speaking with his eyes glued to the sun's eternal downward path in the abyss-like mass of the sky.

"I…I mean, who can blame others for thinkin' me to be insane, really? I must sound so demented, ravin' about my findings, and everyone thinks so. I can tell just by the looks I get whenever I open my mouth, the snickers behind folded hands. I keep blamin' their 'uncreative minds,' but…maybe it is I who is the true problem? Perhaps, my curiosity, my dream, is truly just a fantasy of a crazed man?"

All his words came straight from the darkest parts of his mind, where all his self-doubt and criticism resided. He had long learned to tuck it all away in order to keep the people around him from worrying so much about how he felt about his life. Men, boys, males, whatever…are supposed to be strong for people around them, right? That's what he'd been told; that he should be supporting young people and women more than himself. And he understood that completely. Children's and women's emotions were always valid, and they should be addressed. But so should his emotions, right? His feelings, his mental health, they shouldn't be downplayed or ignored just because he's an adult man, right? To think of it…he rarely even thought about what was tucked away in that dark place in his consciousness, but he needed to say something about it, or he felt his body was going to explode.

And he figured Hemera wouldn't understand, but at the same time, she would.

And sometimes, that perfect balance of uncertainty and comfort was just what he needed to feel sure of himself. He continued with a deep breath, while Hemera just stood, silent (a rare thing), listening, her eyes not moving from the other's teetering form, watching him in stillness.

"I don't want people to pity me. M'not stupid. M'not a young child with a broken knee. I've had no tragedy strike me recently. I don't want them to see me as someone to feel sorry for. 'Oh, look, there he goes again, poor thing.' The way they talk when they see me. The way they treat me like I'm some sort of tickin' bomb or some sort of nasty animal that lugs along harrowing diseases. It…it…makes me feel like another species. Like a foreigner in my own home, unbidden in my own home. It pains me. I feel insignificant. Unheard. I feel like…like nobody understands what I'm even sayin' right now, even as I speak to you."

He looked back down at Hemera to meet her eyes yet again. She was simply observing him with a slightly tilted head, a small stick in her hands forgotten as she listened. She seemed to comprehend most of it, but her eyebrows were slightly furrowed. With confusion? Worry? He sighed and patted the top of her head with a small smile, an attempt at comfort.

"Y'don't have to understand my words, little one. I don't think anyone really can."

Hemera shifted next to him for a good few minutes, as if silently going over what he'd said to her. She finally broke away from him, shrugging as she plodded over to a small mud-like house she'd been building prior to this new topic, and acquired another stick, tossing the old one away. She snapped it in half, absentmindedly, just playing around with whatever she could find to busy herself as she spoke, as if she were some kind of therapist who knew him in and out.

"Well…why do you care?"

His brow furrowed at her statement. He didn't know if she was trying to prove something, switch topics, or take up space. Or all three.

"…elaborate."

"Why do you care, huh? They're all just dumb, anyway. Bullies. Bullies never go anywhere in life, that's what you always said to me. So why are you ignoring what you said? That's…rude to yourself, you know! And to me!"

She spoke as if she were stating some sort of law, an obvious one that everyone knew. And it probably was among children under ten. An unspoken rule of thumb amongst the younger generation.

He never understood kids, because he never really understood anyone. It wasn't that he found it difficult to strike up a conversion.

People just seemed so distant to him. Other people with a whole other life, a whole other personality…. It just made him feel weird. He didn't understand why, and when he didn't understand something, he often avoided it. Not Hemera, though. She was different, in a way. She wasn't a pleasant, obedient child who always did as they were asked and cried if someone tried to start a fight. She wasn't a bratty, insolent, hot-headed child who'd be the one starting fights, rushing over to some unsuspecting child and swinging right at their left eye. No, she was a child who'd make the older children listen to her, turn children younger than her into some sort of loyal followers who she'd address as 'smallers,' roll around in mud until she looked like the mud itself, and then walk up to him like the most innocent being in the world.

She wasn't an easy child at all. But that's what intrigued him so much. She was difficult. So she understood him.

Hemera pointed the stick, which was broken in half and only strung together by a small bit of bark, at the man, not unlike a teacher instructing a particularly difficult child.

"People who are mean are always gonna be mean and never amount to anything bigger. Brother thinks so too. He never says that to them, but I know he thinks it too. He just won't say it, but I know he hates them."

She was always so unequivocal. It made the corners of the man's mouth tug upwards a bit.

"Does he?" he inquired, raising an eyebrow at her words.

Her brother was a very clement soul. He found it hard to imagine him being capable of truly hating anyone. All he'd ever seen her brother do to 'difficult' neighbors was wish them a good day in a stiff voice. Nothing more than that. Her brother did not anger easily, and he knew that well. If he truly hated someone simply because they were impertinent to him, that made him a bit flustered. He felt like some kind of protected damsel.

He didn't quite like that.

Hemera just nodded at his question, looking at him as if he were as dense as a pile of dirt, her tone huffy as she tossed her braid over her shoulder, like a noble who'd been unimpressed by a performance. The man's smile only widened. So much insolence in such a small package. Though, he didn't mind. Sass complimented cheekiness quite well, and oftentimes, that was what had strengthened their bond. And Hemera had always been one to criticize or point out conundrums. Her brother used to say that before Hemera could talk, she could judge people. He wouldn't have been flummoxed if it was proven to be true. A smile like hers was always nothing but trouble and impertinence, but it was hard not to just laugh it off around her. That's just the aura Hemera gave off. With her gap-toothed grin whenever she'd smile, her round cheeks that always puffed out when she ate or pouted, and the way she'd change the way she stumbled and marched every time she took more than seven steps made people forget how much of a wrecking ball she could be.

I mean, she was the whole reason why their next door neighbor Yebei's garden suddenly looked like some sort of plant-crime scene. Oh, that had been heinous. He had gotten his head whacked with a wooden spoon by a woman younger than him, and she'd scolded him on and on about how hard she had worked on her precious plants and how he was so damn lucky there was a child in his company. He'd been so sore headed that she was punishing him for something done by a child he wasn't even related to, that the young woman was also so damn lucky Hemera was beside him, looking up at him with a giggle she was trying to mask, and a small look of partial guilt. He had trudged home grumbling as many profanities he could, while Hemera skipped delightedly beside him, getting off scot-free, because he had been too cross to punish her.

"Yeah. He'd peek through the windows when you'd come home, and the neighbor would say mean stuff to you, and he'd say the word you said when you broke your foot."

"Oh my."

Hemera dusted herself off and lobbed away the stick, huffing as she spoke to the man with a tone of superiority and nonchalance, as if she—a little girl of eight years old—was the one in charge of him.

"Yeah. And he tolded me not to ever be like how the neighbors were being. I told Brother over and over, I could punch the guy right in his big stupid face so he wouldn't bully anyone anymore, but he just tolded me to hush, and go say hi to you, and wash my hands because you'd be dirty from a day out."

She scoffed, as if being told to wash her hands was the filthiest insult she had ever heard.

"But I know it's just because he thinks I'm too small to punch him. But that won't be forever and ever! One day I'll be big, and I'll beat up that stupid guy, and he'll be too scared to be mean! And I'll be in charge of his sorry little face, and he'll kiss my shoes!"

She boasted contemptuously as she took his hand and continued to stare at him with her bright silver eyes. Those eyes that pierced his soul every time he merely glanced at them. How undemanding it was for her to influence him with them, for her to tug at his heartstrings with an unembellished blink. Her charm was so much like her older brother's. Unintentional, but oh God, was it effective. It was like someone had wrested his heart out but then bequeathed him a new one, rearranged his whole soul, remodeled every opinion he'd ever retained. And he had absolutely no objections.

"It's lick your shoes, Hemera, not kiss."

"Whatever."

She paused.

"I don't think you're that crazy, anyway," Hemera said with a nod, as if he'd come to her to plead some innocence for being stark raving mad and she was substantiating that. Though, it didn't concern him now. He finally felt better. He smiled and squeezed her hand in response, not knowing how else to word how he felt, before scooping her compact little body up into his arms and then placing her meticulously on top of his shoulders, her hands grasping his neck, his holding her shins so she wouldn't fall. He grinned up at her as he started trekking again.

"Thank you, little one. Now, you wanna join this crazy guy on another trip?"

# The Village of Silence

Aurum rouses with a sudden jolt and in a cold sweat. That dream…it seemed more like some kind of memory. The illusions of chains, of water, of drowning.

Chains.

He instantly scrutinizes his wrists, both of them, inspecting them all over. No chains bind him. No marks of them ever even being on his supple skin. But, how? They were just there! And he was underwater, and—

His head swivels like a chair with wheels, hurriedly surveying his surroundings. No water. There are what look like willow trees dancing beautifully in the lukewarm gust that passes the saccharin smell of flowers and summer in through the air, and viridescent grass with a vague tawny glow all around him. But the small pool is not visible anymore.

*Have you already forgotten?*

No, he hasn't. He thinks he hasn't. Has he?

Nothing seems veracious anymore. He gapes around anew and discerns this time that the colors that had seemed so vibrant before are now duller. Things seem soulless and dreary.

The young man from the water is gone.

Aurum wonders why he was in the water. Why hadn't he gotten out sooner? The faint shimmer of his skin glistens in the fast-fading light. It would be foolish to jump into the water in the first place if it were just a shallow puddle. And he seemed to have known more about it then Aurum, so why would he have been there if he knew it would trap him under?

Something is certainly not right. It can't be right. The air he breathes now feels fake, like some kind of cheap replica. As he arises with the hankering to find others to ask about his encounter with the idiosyncratic individual, he feels light. Like he is dreaming. The sky is still orange with the color of sunset. He turns to try and find others like himself. Or at least people. Maybe they'll understand.

The grass is silvery and it slightly shimmers as he walks further through the strange world. The trees tower above him as he explores, the fast-fading sunlight leaking in from gaps between the leaves, like liquid warmth pooling onto the ground. Everything glistens, like water has coated every last inch of the world around him. This is truly one of the most peculiar things ever. It feels like a sickeningly beautiful fever dream. As he travels, he tries to scope out where it looks the least natural, hoping that means people have been through there. He finds himself heading west. Perhaps on the west side of this place there is some kind of civilization. He doesn't care how big or small. The people don't even have to be kind. He just needs to find someone who doesn't make him rethink everything he's ever known about himself, his life, and his origins. Hopefully, the west is the best chance of finding people.

He is right.

A little village appears. It is shrouded in a thin layer of silvery mist, though it is different from the fog masking the other part of the woodland that he had originally found. This fog does not injure him as he passes through it, instead giving him a small feeling of comfort as he inhales the air around it. The homes are made of a pale, splintery, gray wood, and they almost resemble whole trees in a way.

A warm light casts a shadow of the houses, making the whole scene seem like a painting. There is nobody outside. Aurum is alone in the village, it seems. Most of the houses seem desolate and abandoned, and they radiate an unwelcoming aura. He is almost intimidated. The houses loom with imposing shadows, softly curved walls turned sharp when mirrored, and they cast a dark spot-on Aurum when he passes them. He notices that a lot of houses have unique features, even if they all have similar structure and architecture style. Most of the roofs of these houses are in the shape of a small point, slanted and fat. The materials look to be kinds of leaves and wood held up by pale beams that boast a few soft patches of moss and fungus. A few cylinder-shaped mushrooms form a tiny staircase up a window, which is just a circular hole carved into the wood. There are no curtains in several of the windows he peers into, but a few have a silk sheet to place in front of the windows. On the outside, some have gardens. Others have neat little arrays of stone in the front, and some even have what could resemble small dolls and blocks for children splayed out in front of or behind their houses. A doll Aurum spots over to the left of a smaller house looks to be made of pressed leaves and fabric woven together to form what vaguely resembles a tiny girl. A common theme he begins to notice, though, is that there is no more sound inside these fascinating homes than outside of them. He pulls his head away from the opening of a rather small house's window and looks over toward the further side of the seemingly desolate village. Another abode catches his eyes.

There, in the very far corner of this small and once-cozy village, he sees a house a bit bigger than the others, with what looks like a telescope made from wood, leaves, and tempered glass on the roof, along with what looks like some kind of supplies. He walks towards the door of the house, curious as to what exactly awaits him inside. Something bright gets his attention next to the door— painting. The painting is done in differing styles, as the three people depicted in it have contrasting appearances.

The first one is a tall figure with an expression of joviality and warm cream-colored hair and a red streak painted through it. The next figure is a shorter one with mahogany-brown hair and light almond skin. Their face depicts a calmer and warmer smile, and the art style is more flowy. The third one is a child's drawing of a very small figure, one with blonde hair and blobs of white for finery. Aurum smiles to himself. It approximates a family self-portrait, almost. How gratifying. He focuses back on the door after a moment. There is no door handle, so he has no other option except to push it open. Though, that would be intruding, wouldn't it?

Aurum bites his lip, looking around at the surrounding houses. Each one looks abandoned, desolate, so perhaps there is no difference with this one either? Aurum doesn't want to risk getting something thrown into his eye the moment he takes one step onto the interior floor, so he tentatively raps on the frail wood. No answer. He calls out lightly.

"Excuse me? Uh, is anyone home?"

Once more, there is no answer. Aurum coughs to try and intervene in the silence that's settled over him, before he tries again.

"Well…I'm just going to come in. Just for a second. Maybe you're uh…deaf, or something."

He nudges open the door as quietly as he can, mostly because making a loud noise somewhere so quiet feels almost wrong.

Inside, he can see that the whole house has a silvery hue with a light bit of a marmalade tint. There is an unlit fire below a pot and one bed or couch…whatever it is, in a corner. The couch looks more like just places where silk is placed carefully to make a comfortable and congenial area to sit. This place may have been home to someone once, but now it seems almost forsaken. Aurum allows himself to look over a small basket in the corner, chock-full of what looks like a peculiar kind of fruit. The fruit is a pearl gray, slightly shiny from interior juices having leaked out from its shell of soft flesh. Perhaps someone has harvested them too harshly, Aurum muses to himself. However, as he adjusts his perspective from the basket, he is able to glimpse the spots of oozing mold and smell the unmistakable fragrance of decay, and he quickly concedes that it wouldn't matter how they were picked, they were long rotted.

A faint, padding, slightly repetitive noise from outside startles him. A faint pap pap pap of something moving against grass, against the earth. Something gentle, yet strong enough to allow the ground below to alert the surrounding areas.

There are footsteps.

*Is your guilt finding you?*

Guilt?

The footsteps draw near, and the door opens with a quiet creak. And as the door opens, it reveals a person. It's another young man. He is wearing a similar light-colored outfit to Aurum's own, it's loose and reaches his ankles. It's like a robe, almost. A white scarf is draped around his neck and hangs a bit in the back, sagging. Under the light scarf is a top that consists of several woven patterns, like one would see on quilts or blankets, in grays, whites, and beiges. The bottom resembles a skirt in a way, but it parts into two pieces near his knees and grazes the floor slightly as he shifts his posture. It's a tan color and has noticeable wrinkles. The entire outfit overall is torn and faded, and some pieces scatter as the wind blows. He looks entirely like any other person would.

Except Aurum cannot see his face clearly. He can see his expression, his mouth, his eyes, all of that…and yet he can't see his face the way he has seen others. When Aurum tries to observe a feature, his vision blurs. His whole face smudges like wet paint on a canvas. Aurum grows impatient as he tries hard to make out his face. It's impossible to see him clearly. He squints his eyes, but that only blurs it more. It's useless. It's like in a dream, where everyone's face is there, and he knows who they are but if he didn't know people had distinct faces and features, he wouldn't know from looking at him.

*But do you even deserve to see him again?*

He stands there, looking at Aurum as though he isn't even there. Aurum thinks he must not notice him, but as the man begins to talk to him, that thought is cast away.

"So. You have returned."

Returned? Returned from what? From where? He gives Aurum no explanation, and just stares at him as if awaiting an answer, leaving him muddled. Has he encountered him before?

*So, you have forgotten. Foolish.*

No, not foolish if Aurum's never met him. So how could he have forgotten him if he's never seen him? And he'd have known if he had met him on a previous occasion. Wouldn't he?

"Is everything all right?"

Aurum glances up to see his face again. It doesn't change one bit. It is impossible to look at. It's like a watercolor painting that's started dripping and smearing. This is a dream, then. That's the only real logical explanation. That's why his face is blurred so oddly.

"Everything…everything is quite all right. No concern is needed, thank you," Aurum says courteously, although he is lying both to himself and this strange person before him. The person tilts his head, and for a moment he is gone, disappearing almost like the flickering of a candle flame.

Aurum realizes how much like a dream this man seems.

Distant. Faded. Fragile.

"I do apologize. Perhaps I'm losing myself," he says, his tone laced with a note of sorrow, but Aurum cannot distinguish why. Mistaken? Losing himself? What does he mean? There's a long pause, a tense moment in the atmosphere. He says nothing briefly, merely staring into space as though nothing around them is important to him, as if everything just…doesn't matter to him anymore. He starts to make a few sounds, and it takes Aurum a long time to realize that the sounds are some kind of hoarse and choked chortle.

"I really…don't know…"

The person seems almost morbid now. Aurum decides asking about this might upset him and leaves the conversation at that.

However, before anything can be further spoken, a cacophonous noise startles him. It almost sounds like water gurgling. He opens his mouth to speak, but suddenly, he's choking.

Aurum is drowning in nothing.

His vision darkens abruptly and he discerns the thunderous blare once again, but it sounds like the rising of a wave right before it crashes into the shore. Closer…closer—

Scintillating light pierces through the darkness.

And he's inside of that minute house again.

He's sprawled on the floor, head in his hands, gripping his hair as if he is going to wrest it out of his scalp. Aurum doesn't even recall moving. His face heats up in perturbation.

Oh, God.

Now that man saw him looking like some sort of insane fool.

Wait. Aurum sits up and looks around in pure bewilderment. Where did the man go?

One second, he was sitting across from him on the floor, looking like the sun had died, and now, he's just…gone! Aurum whips his gaze around the room, searching for him before he freezes and realizes…the room. It has changed almost entirely.

The room has morphed, as though it had completely transformed into something entirely separate from the original. The fruit in the basket is not rotten, and the broken and splintered wood that once made up the walls had faded, and the walls appear to be in peak condition. Sunlight streams through windows, illuminating the room with an orange tint, one that feels comforting and homey. Everything seems perfect, really. What's more, the fire is lit, and something bubbles in a pot above the fireplace.

All the walls seem to stand proudly, strong and stable, their rough, bark-like appearance contrasting with their smooth and shiny surface giving the room a very polished look. The ceiling is covered wall-o-wall in tiny vine-like foliage and small white flowers with reaching petals that end in the shape of a snake's tongue hang limply from these green wires of nature. A sweet scent emits from their radiant blossoms. Some are still noticeably buds, their bright white dresses stained sage and yellow, folded inwards with the promise of a beautiful awakening. These flowery vines snake their way up to a small stairway toward the far corner of the room that Aurum had failed to notice earlier. The wood there looks slightly worn, and it is obvious that the stairs had been used either quite frequently by one person, or quite a few times by several. He cannot see what the upstairs floor has to offer, but he can imagine it probably consists of a few bedrooms or washrooms. The room he is in as of now still has most of its original placement, but there is more furniture and decor. To his left, he notices a few cabinets and other useful things to store items in. There is a large armoire—or is it a chifforobe of some kind? He can't tell. The doors are shut and locked. Though the beautiful silver-like handles beckon him to open them, or find a key, he resists and continues to observe. A small wooden bucket of water is placed near the fireplace, which is tucked away in a corner near where quite a few dried flowers and herbs hang, perfuming the area even more than the flowers above his head. It almost makes the air around him overwhelming, and he becomes gradually aware that his eyes are watering. He wipes them on his sleeve dismissively. There is a table about six feet away from these herbs and the fire, near a large window that allows the golden sun rays of the evening to pour into the room and give the entire place a feeling of peace. Three chairs are arranged at the table, all empty. He keeps a mental note to himself about this number. Must be a family of three. Or three roommates.

To his right are a few baskets of what looks like wood, for the fire that is merrily stirring in its place below the pot in the corner of the room, and some small trinkets like rolled-up pieces of parchment paper and small jars of flora and rocks and even a few fireflies. Aurum tilts his head at the small, gleaming insects. How peculiar.

Aurum turns around at a sudden grunt of frustration to find him, that man he was talking to earlier, on his tiptoes in front of a wooden cabinet—an open one this time, with transparent doors. It is filled with jars containing who-knows-what, reaching for something that looks like salt, but is a bit more warm-colored, almost like it had been dyed in peach juice. He is still wearing what he was before, the light clothes that resembled plain bedsheets, but it's a bit tighter on him, revealing a healthy figure with slight curves on their legs and upper body. His arms look toned, but his legs even more so, and Aurum can guess he probably walks around a lot. Or he just stands on his tiptoes all day, like he's doing now. On top of the fact that his attire is tighter and looks less shabby, it is also spotless and pristine, like new, and the sleeves aren't frayed. Not a bit of the attire is torn or dirty, and what shocks Aurum the most is his face. Aurum can see every feature.

There's an apparent and faded scar ghosting over his lips, a jagged line vertically placed in the corner of his mouth. It's tiny enough to probably be from an injury he'd gotten at a very young age, one that wasn't serious, but enough to leave a mark. Or it could be one given to him later in his years, perhaps a gift from a rival. Aurum momentarily finds himself fascinated with this blemish on the man's lips, which are pursed slightly.

Aurum is speechless. It is as if the other version of the room, and the person he had seen mere seconds ago never existed.

"Weren't you just…on the other side of the room?"

The young man turns around in stupefaction, his eyes opening wider, a great contrast from his squint of utter concentration. His eyes are copper-gray, and his eyelashes are fairly long and brush up against his cheeks as he blinks. They have a square shape, one that turns into a faint oval as he lowers his eyelids. He has noticeable eye bags, but he doesn't look exhausted, only a bit stressed or maybe tired, but not sleep deprived or anything. It goes without saying that he did not at all expect to see Aurum standing in the middle of the room, staring straight at him like a hawk watching a mouse.

"I– Huh?"

He stops reaching for the glass and folds his hands in an apprehensive way. He looks Aurum up and down and frowns a little, like Aurum isn't supposed to be there.

Oh wait. He probably isn't.

"Um…"

The man gives Aurum a stare with a raised eyebrow, as if trying to convey some sort of gentle hint, but Aurum doesn't really understand.

Poor thing. Just like a newborn, really.

The copper-eyed man eventually just sighs and places his hands on his hips, stepping forward into the path of sunlight from a nearby window. His fair, light-brown skin seems to glow on his nose and cheeks, and his freckles are more prominent than Aurum had previously seen them, the tiny dots of melanin trailing down his neck and sprinkled on his legs. It was clear he spent much of his time in the sun. His cheeks are slightly plump, yet they complement his jawline perfectly, seeming to give him an aura of maturity, while still keeping a younger look. Aurum can't be sure what to think, as he doesn't know anything of the man's age. His hair is tousled and reaches the base of his neck in the back, still swirly and just barely making the cut of presentable. Somehow, though, he manages to look intimidating.

He's not stern, but he's assertive with Aurum.

"Dare I even ask what you're doing inside of my house?"

Aurum knows that only moments before, they had talked. Aurum knows that. And he knows that, at the time, this man thought he looked familiar, like someone he didn't seem to want to see again. And yet now he seems genuinely puzzled with Aurum's entire existence, like Arum had somehow changed just as much as this strange man and the room had in the span of a second.

"We were having a conversation only minutes ago," Aurum says calmly, hoping he'll think and then say, "Oh yeah, I remember you," and that'll be the end of it. No such luck. The look on his face does not change, so Aurum concludes that trying is pointless.

"Never mind, sorry…I'll leave."

"No, stay. Tell me why you're in my house, please."

"I told you; we were…"

As he begins to explain himself, he turns his gaze upward from the ground and is greeted by the sight of the man turned back around, huffing as he grasps at the air hopelessly for the salt. This man is in no way short, why is this such a challenge for him? Aurum can't take him seriously while he's struggling so much to get that glass jar on the higher shelf. It makes him look significantly smaller than he is, and Aurum's words lessen in volume and confidence the more the man hops in an attempt to grab the glass, his manner nearly mimicking a child's in that situation.

"…Talk…ing…Um, what are you doing?"

The man blinks and pauses before his face flushes in embarrassment. He hops down from the inclined part of the floor he was on and dusts off his clothes.

"I'm trying to make sure everything is in an organized place, since a new addition is being added here."

A new addition? Aurum can only assume he is talking about some kind of home renovation, as the state of the house was cozy, but it certainly seemed a little bit…garish. Was tidying for an addition to one's house a common thing? Perhaps, maybe everyone did it. Maybe it was a special custom.

Back on the matter at hand.

It takes him a while to fully process that he's talking to a person. It's wonderful, really, to finally have someone who responds to your words instead of shoving you head-first into icy water. A real, breathing person, who can see and speak, and—

And then suddenly, everything around him dulls. It's not like previously, where everything was too much. Everything suddenly just stops. His ears ring, the only sound in the swampy silence.

Aurum hears the person beside him say something, hears them call out to him and then feels them grab his shoulder, but his words are drowned out by silence, by ringing, by utter blankness. Aurum reaches out for some kind of surface as he feels his head start to spin, but his fingers catch nothing but the breeze he felt earlier through the window. But now, the wind feels icy cold on his fingertips. For a moment, the cold almost burns, and he cries out. The steady hand on his shoulder is too heavy. It's weighing him down like an anchor, he's sinking into the floor like a man in quicksand.

Breathing. Right, Aurum must breathe. It's like he'd forgotten to.

Aurum's head starts to clear after a few minutes and he realizes he has fallen onto his knees, clutching the sides of his skull. Oh. When he pulled away so violently from the man's hand, which was steadying him, he must have knocked himself off his balance and fell. The pain from earlier must have been him hitting the ground. Speaking of, that same man from before is beside him, and now he looks even more perplexed. Though, now, his expression noticeably shows that he is far more concerned about Aurum's mental state than anything else.

"I…Um. Are you all right? That was…something."

Aurum knows he isn't all right, that he probably should be running away right that moment, but deep down he has the sinking feeling that he cannot run away, that he is stuck here. Aurum lets his hands fall from the sides of his head. If he can't run, at least it is safe here for now.

"Yes."

The words escape from his lips before he can think.

"I'm all right."

# The Promise

The man groaned in frustration, leaning his head back with a huff. For nearly four days, he'd been working himself to the bone for that damn map. How could he have so carelessly dropped it? How could he have allowed such an event? Hemera stood a few feet away from him, tapping her foot, eyebrows raised. It was obvious that the little girl was past all of his moping around, and she made no move to hide her annoyance.

"Come on, we've been looking for that stupid map for almost two hours now. Brother's going to have your head for this. And your siblings, Finy and Prinlin—"

"Fanyu and Priolaine. And they're my cousins, mind you," he responded, moving his head up off of the ground, which he'd been helplessly lying on for a good ten minutes in utter despair at misplacing such a precious item. Of course, the one time he wanted to take Hemera out on some serious adventure, this happens. Now he looked like some kind of wannabe adventurer, attempting to coax his company to follow him for just one more mile. Being that his company was an eight-year-old girl with absolutely no sense of self awareness, it was even more of a hassle. Of course, it isn't as though she hadn't been at his side all day many times before, it was just…

During the last few trips he had taken, which he had spent scouring the forest in and out, hurtling head-first at the mist toward the far end of his village (for which he'd gotten several concerned stares), and jotting down sentence after sentence in one of his many notebooks, he'd notice Hemera had started losing interest. Her constant questions had subsided into the occasional 'I thought you said…' and 'There's supposed to be…' This hadn't bothered him quite as much the first time, but by the fifth day she began nearly every rare question with these, he had started sweating. He didn't want to believe that Hemera was losing hope or faith in him and the beautiful paintings he'd made inside her mind when he told her stories by their fireplace about tall, imposing men who bent the winds with a mere breath, and infinite space where new beings were created everywhere, and all of them different. A faraway land of simply endless opportunity. Not some caged-in village that spat at the idea of his imagination and dreams.

His dazed state was cut short by Hemera's whining.

"Ugh, can't you just make some kinda new map or something?"

"Well, I—"

"And you know this whole place inside and out, so what do you even need that dumb map for? Don't you have a good memory? You told me you did!"

His face heated up at the blatant way he was called out by a girl nearly one-third his age. He had said that, but it was mainly so she would shut up about him remembering what kind of flowers she liked. And of course, he'd remembered that because she'd nagged him about those goddamn moonblooms for nearly a week before he had folded. Truth be told, his memory was just as bad as a newborn's.

Wait, did newborns have a good memory? No, they couldn't have, because nobody remembers infancy. The man frowned at this before he snapped back into reality to return to the current task he faced — attempting to lie to Hemera.

"Y'see…I may have been exaggerating just a teeny tiny, itty bitty little bit?"

He held up his hand with open palms, a sheepish smile curving half his lip up toward his cheek. Although no attempt at innocence would fool Hemera. He knew that better than anything. He was proven right when she huffed, stomping her foot on the grassy soil.

"See! You have a lying problem!"

He blinked in astonishment. Where had that come from? They were talking about some map he had lost! He sputtered out some attempt to protest Hemera's sudden accusation, having no idea how to understand why she was so upset. He didn't have a problem! He hardly ever stretched the truth!

"Hemera—m'sorry, just a little confused here. I don't have any lying problem, where did you—"

"Yes, you do! You keep saying all this fancy stuff about the future and what you're looking for, and all of that, but you're lying! You said you'd prove it to me, and now the map is lost! Lost? Why is it lost now, of all times? You've always had it there, and now, suddenly, it's gone! You lied! I know this trick, you lied to me!"

Hemera's mood had changed at such a quick pace that he was sure he had missed something along the lines of translation. He took in what the young girl was saying, noticing how disgruntled she looked. Her eyes were suddenly brimming with the threat of tears, small fists clenched firmly at her sides, feet adjusted into a defensive stance. He knew he seemed dishonest with her, and he knew all along she was losing faith in his words, but he had never expected an outburst from her regarding such a thing. His face softened, and he carefully got up off the ground, making his way over to the sniveling girl that he had come to love despite all of her little tantrums and quirks. He kneeled down beside her, and while she still stared at him unflinchingly, he saw her lip quiver and he let out a sigh.

"Yeah, I know this looks real bad, little one. 'm sorry, I really am."

He began cautiously, testing the waters for what type of approach she'd reject or accept. It was hard to tell, though, as nothing in her expression dimmed. He sucked in a breath and some confidence, continuing.

"…y'don't hafta come on all my little trips, y'know. I'm perfectly fine goin' alone. 'm all grown up. I can handle it. I won't be upset at all if you don't wanna keep coming with me just to be disappointed in the end. Even though I still firmly believe that one day, I'll come home and make you happy, that day may take a while, and I don't want you wastin' all the precious time y've got."

She sniffled at his words, drinking them in obediently, although she didn't appear to be any happier.

"So, I can't go on any more adventures?"

"Not for a while, unfortunately, little one. I think it's best if you head back with your brother and spend some time with him. He misses you. Then again, I don't care if you wanna spend your time with the other kids again. I know y'miss 'em, and you need to start talkin' with kids your own age again."

Hemera let a pout grace her lips, her bottom lip sticking out as a small tear raced down her cheek.

"But the other kids are stupid."

He smiled at her, wiping away her tears with his hands, thumbs wiping at the corners of her big, starry eyes. He kissed her forehead.

"Well then, make 'em into your soldiers, my lady. Soldiers don't need brains so long as they've got someone tellin' them what to do."

She giggled half-heartedly as he pressed his lips to her temple, and she gave him a watery grin.

"Will you be my soldier, then?"

The man barked out a laugh, ruffling her hair.

"Very funny. I'll be your knight."

# The Husk

Aurum had been quite embarrassed after the little incident he'd had not even two minutes into a conversation with some random man who's house he'd intruded upon. In response, the young man, who introduced himself formally as Osuna, had only waved it off and helped him over to a table, where he had given him a small cup of water and a pat on the back. They had chatted for quite some time, attempting to clear up the situation at hand. Aurum had explained how he'd come to the house, deliberately leaving out the details of there being some kind of shadow-like man there previously, and the sudden shift in the atmosphere of the house. In turn, Osuna told him it was all fine, so long as Aurum had no ill will against him, which the latter quickly agreed with. After that, Osuna had questioned the incident, which Aurum had no response to. Proper introductions were said, or really as proper as they could've been, in Aurum's case, and, after deeming Aurum to be of no threat, Osuna insisted he stay for as long as he would like, as it sounded like Aurum had nowhere else he needed to be, and nowhere else he was really able to go.

Osuna seemed to either have no sort of survival instinct in the slightest or the kindest heart since the beginning of time, but Aurum was not exactly complaining about having a place to stay. He quickly came to the realization that Osuna may have just seen him as too pathetic to truly cause any harm, as that's essentially how he felt. Aurum had resisted the offer first, not wanting to intrude, but caved in once he remembered he truly didn't have anywhere else to go.

Currently, Aurum is conversing with Osuna. It's about three or four days after they had first met. Or at least, Osuna told him it had been a few days. Aurum isn't exactly sure. Everything either seems to stretch on eerily or vanish entirely in a blink of an eye. Aurum sits across from Osuna as the latter rambles, while occasionally pausing to look over at the boiling pot in the corner of the room, snug inside of the hearth with the promise of some sort of scrumptious concoction within—or so he said. Aurum is listening, although his concentration is wavering. His mind bubbles just as the large pot does, questions coming to the surface as easily as breathing. He interrupts Osuna briefly, shyly raising his hand, to which the other ceases his talking and nods.

"Oh, yes, I'm sorry. How rude of me, yapping on and on…"

He stands up from the table with a small grunt, still talking to Aurum as he heads over to the fireplace. Aurum notices no sort of limp or stutter in his movements, so he assumes that the reasoning for all the huffing and groaning the other had been doing was either due to some kind of exhaustion or fatigue. Perhaps he simply found everything to be a chore. Aurum can sympathize. The whole house seemed to be empty, save for him. A lonely life, surely. Aurum adjusts his position in the slightly uncomfortable wooden chair, before he lets out a feeble laugh as if to distract from his delayed answer.

"Yes, yes…I mean– no! No, you're not yapping."

The sudden panic in Aurum's voice as he realizes what he had said is mighty amusing to Osuna, and he chuckles good-naturedly at his guest's mistake. Aurum almost deflates as he sees this, thankful that the other is not cross with him. If he were kicked out, he'd truly have no other place to go if he couldn't find a way home. Not that this place is a permanent stay, of course. Aurum redeems himself tentatively, starting out cautiously and gingerly.

"Well…what I meant to say was that I do have something to ask and to say…if that's all right with you, of course…yes? Okay then."

He confirms with a nod at the other's encouraging smile.

"I wanted to know…what do you do all day? Just…sit around and tidy and cook? It seems rather…dull, but it's all I've seen you do for four whole days."

Aurum doesn't want to accidentally insult his host, so he pauses every now and then between words he is less than excited to say. He coughs occasionally as well, as if to break some kind of silence, even if he's in the middle of talking. The logic of Aurum's speech doesn't make all that much sense, it's more like a cry for help, but his goal is reached, and Osuna doesn't look one bit offended. Osuna shrugs his shoulders.

"Well, yes, I don't have much else to do as of the present. You know, I get really annoyed with how unorganized things are, and it gets to me greatly when they pile up. So, I suppose I've just been…trying to get things together, is all. I mean, everything should be where it belongs, right?"

Aurum hums thoughtfully at the words, contemplating them.

"I guess so. But sometimes, you must let things find their own sort of rhythm, right? If you just keep things in the same places, you'll get bored with the way your house looks."

Aurum jokes lightheartedly. But as he turns to face the other, Osuna is simply staring back at him, blankly. Scrutinizing. Aurum shifts nervously at those eyes staring into his own. Had he misspoken? Said something the other found condescending? Perhaps commenting on how someone could get bored with his house sounded rude…

"Uh…Osuna? You all right?" he asks him tentatively, leaning forward.

Osuna merely blinks, as if he'd been zoned out during the exchange, then his eyes shift back to their previous warmth, glancing over Aurum's face with curiosity.

"Hm? Oh! Yes, yes, I'm all right."

He responds cheerfully, rubbing his under eyes with a faint smile. He looks awfully tired, the light brown under his eyes mixing with an undertone of pale lavender and sickly blue-gray. Not that he looks sick, per se, but Aurum can see exhaustion lacing his features. Must be from the constant tidying and nitpicking and such that he had been doing. Aurum hadn't really seen the man take a break since he'd arrived. Even when he'd been ushered up the staircase to sleep, he'd never once seen the latter in bed, not even the next morning. He'd only been up bright and early, with a cheery grin on his lips and a small, steaming cup in his hands that smelled faintly like citrus. Aurum looks pityingly at Osuna rubbing his eyes, long sleeves quivering with the motion. Aurum's expression of pity slightly fades, giving way to a frown. Osuna seems to almost fade as he shakes. Something still isn't quite right. People don't flicker out or waver. They have a solid outline and defining structure. This man has the overall appearance and movements of a shadow.

Aurum must get home. And aren't other people his best shot? But is this wisp of a person really who he is seeking for help? No. He can't be. Aurum sighs.

"I think you should sleep."

Osuna perks up slightly at the sudden suggestion, raising an eyebrow.

"But I—"

"Nope. No to anything you were about to say. You look utterly spent, and I don't think it's a good idea for you to keep pushing yourself if you have nothing left to push from. Your little chores or tasks aren't going anywhere, believe me. And you've been working on them all day, every day, for two days straight. I think you deserve a break."

Aurum doesn't add on the fact that Osuna looks like he is practically disappearing from how tired he appears. Maybe it is just a mirage of some sort, paranoia from how stressed he is about his entire predicament. After all, disorientation can cause hallucinations. He doesn't want to add any more stress onto Osuna, who stops talking and only nods in resignation. Aurum manages to catch a slight glint of relief in his eyes.

A few nights ago, Osuna had shown Aurum everything that lay upstairs, of which there was only one room, which was a rather large bedroom. Osuna had mentioned it had other uses besides sleeping, and Aurum had told him he had not come over for that kind of assistance. The other had just stared at him blankly for several awkward seconds.

Now, Aurum is the one leading Osuna up the creaky wooden steps and guiding him through the doorway. The room itself is not at all disappointing. In the corner, a bed made from what looks like piled silks on a hammock. The hammock itself is a soft baby blue color (thank the good Lord above—Aurum was growing sick of the yellows and whites and oranges that just seemed to make up the entire world) with small swirly patterns of lighter and darker indigo shades. It's around three feet wide and just long enough for him to squeeze into. It was obviously made for someone smaller, perhaps a very young child, or a short juvenile. Either way, it's not quite made for someone his size, but it's not impossible to fit into.

The ropes on it are strung on the bottom and top and look like pale ivy vines that snake up to the ceiling and then pool there. They hold the hammock surprisingly well, and there isn't even any small creaking as he lies in the hanging bed. The silks are white and surprisingly temperate and congenial, encasing Osuna like a smooth cocoon, as Aurum helps him into the bed with a bit of struggle.

Aurum peers at him.

"This bed isn't yours, I take it?"

Osuna chuckles warmly.

"No, it's not. But it's one of the coziest beds in the house, and I always wondered if I could fit in here. Turns out, it's a bit of a squeeze, but doable."

It isn't quite what he is used to, Aurum can tell, but the silks are soft and light, and Aurum bets they feel marvelous on his skin, perhaps because they share similar properties, cushiony and smooth.

Aurum takes a good look around the room as he assists Osuna with climbing into the bed more comfortably. On his side, here's a rather great bookshelf filled to the brim with disarrayed notebooks and books, papers spilling out from overflowing leather capsules of knowledge all lined up somewhat neatly. Some have a few symbols on the covers, others have the covers ripped right off. There are pens and papers strewn out on a corner table near the small angular window to his left side, and various scribbles can be seen on the parchment. On top of that, there are a few little paper chains and dolls hanging from the ceiling, each one looks very yellowed, and a few wooden dolls splayed out near a corner. Aurum can see two distinct ones, looking like they were the last to be played with. They are about the size of his hand, and these dolls have long, beautiful hair, and modest dresses. They have no facial features except for two carved out circles that resemble eyes. Odd figures, but not too odd that he can't see a little girl having a grand time with them. Despite the childlike atmosphere, the overall feeling of the room itself makes it easy to adjust from a tense mood to a rather at ease one. Aurum smiles at Osuna lightly.

"Goodnight then, Osuna. I hope you feel better once you're rested," he says smoothly, fixing one of the hammock's ropes ends just to check that it is secure. After about thirty seconds of this, his brow furrows as he becomes aware of the lack of response. Osuna really fell asleep that easily? He must have really been tired. Aurum picks at a thin part in the rope as he tries again. Perhaps he was too quiet. He was trying to be softer just so the other would be able to slip into unconsciousness faster, but maybe he'd been too quiet, and Osuna had assumed it to be nothing, or simply imagination.

"Goodnight, Osuna."

Still nothing. No rustling of the blankets, no faint breath of acknowledgement, no mumbles of confirmation. Aurum looks up from the rope he is messing with to confront the other, but any words die on his lips.

Osuna is sitting straight up in bed, in the same position Aurum had seen him in before he'd turned his back to fix the rope. He hasn't moved one inch. His eyes are open, but they are glassy and unblinking, staring past Aurum, past everything. Aurum pales at the sight, unsure if he should be worried for Osuna or not. He hesitantly draws back up to his full height and pokes at Osuna's cheek.

"Osuna?"

The man's head lolls onto his shoulder and his body goes limp.

Aurum's feeling can only be described as breathless. Completely still and silent. Unsure what to say, unsure what to do. There's only one question in his head.

"What the hell?"

What just happened?

What's happening?

Why is this happening??

"Right…help."

He mutters to himself, forcing his feet, which feel glued to the floor, to move, to walk.

"I have to…find something to help."

Aurum stays rooted in place for a while, just gazing at the scene before him, before he rushes out of the room and down the stairs in such speed that he is almost sure one of the steps breaks as he hops off of it.

His head whips around, silver irises frantically scanning and searching for the door he had entered from. He knew it was somewhere around…there! He stumbles toward it rapidly, tripping over his own feet, not even bothering to try and push the door, or search for a door handle, and just running into the door at full speed so it just shoves open, wood creaking noisily in protest to such brutishness. Aurum hurries out into the surrounding landscape, stopping once he is a good ten feet from the house.

He needs to catch his breath. He needs to think. He needs to get help for Osuna, for himself, for everything…

What has even happened? Osuna probably just passed out or something, why is he reacting so harshly?

Aurum slows his breathing, his frantic heartbeats slowing to a lighter speed, just faint nervous pattering. There is nothing but trees and nature behind him, and once the sound of his thundering heart rate fades from his ear drums, it dims to utter nothingness. The silence hurts like a slap to the face. He is…alone. He lets out a long exhale of a breath and looks up, hair that still isn't his messy and in his face, as he lets out ragged breaths. He feebly attempts to gather his thoughts.

What to do? Where to go next?

The village around him is tranquil and quiet, and nothing could have possibly caused any harm to Osuna. Aurum tries to remind himself of this. But something about its atmosphere has changed, and a tugging instinct urges him to walk away. There is no denying it now.

The naive little man is no longer safe here.

# The First Sign

Yureni was absolutely exhausted as he stumbled through the doorframe of the pale wooden house. Although, he knew that it was his own fault anyway, he could barely stand up after all those continuous hours of searching, searching, searching…

Lean copper arms caught his body as he fell over forward due to his exhaustion from walking for three hours, and a soft voice tsked in his ear, the tone a teacher would use when referring to a late student. All too familiar with this situation, Yureni carefully wrapped his arms around the other's slightly smaller—although, not the least bit less muscular—figure that was propping him up, hoping perhaps a more pleasant and undemanding approach would soothe the other's vexation. He didn't even have to look at his face to know that the look of it was as plain as day.

"Hello, Osuna."

He started out sheepishly, trying to somehow circumvent any sternness from his lover, if that were even possible. Like any pair of lovers, he and Osuna had differing opinions on the other's curfew and behavior. Osuna had given Yureni a very reasonable time frame for curfew whenever Yureni stayed over at his home for a day or a week or a month, solely because of the scheduling of meals, chores, and Hemera's bedtime. It was a good schedule that Yureni had no objections to and usually no problem following.

Except for earlier that day when he'd been able to obtain one of the most exciting leads he'd gotten since he first started his quest. He had pleaded with Osuna like a party-going teenager for a later schedule change, so Osuna had begrudgingly agreed on the condition that he come back soon. He'd promised he'd be back home to Osuna in an hour.

Six hours ago.

Osuna simply gave him the same look he'd give Hemera when she asked him too many questions on a hard day (thank God he hadn't gotten the same lecture she had). He was not impressed and it showed. Osuna was a very kind and gentle soul, always willing to help out with the tasks of others, and never one to accuse or argue over small matters. He was a very calm and collected person, but he was also very— How could Yureni put it? — encouraging, when it came to others being as altruistic to him as he was to them. Although he was extremely even-tempered and caring, like anyone else, he had limits to this aura of collective peace. His patience had a point where it ran thin.

Timing and waiting for too long was one of these points.

Osuna let out a sigh as he hoisted Yureni to his feet. He tucked a lock of dark hair behind his ear and crossed his arms. Yureni always noted how this really made him look more like somebody's mother when their son didn't follow basic instructions. That made him feel a lot more bashful than he already was. Osuna spoke in a warning tone, and Yureni had to check and make sure Osuna didn't have a wooden spoon clasped in his hand.

"Yureni, we talked about this. You know I worry. I thought something had happened to you," Osuna whispered to him, tone more upset than angry or stern, which was about ten times worse than if he'd hollered.

Yureni nodded in response, ducking his head in humiliation. He knew he'd been scatterbrained with that kind of thing a lot recently, but he just got so wrapped up in what he was doing that it had become knackering to put things on pause. Inspiration spurts came to him at the worst possible times. Though, now he felt abashed for putting his interests and beliefs above his own partner.

"I know, I'm sorry, Osuna," he replied meekly.

Yureni was both taller and louder than Osuna, and he knew his way better around physical things, but whenever Osuna took a firm tone with him, he usually just folded and allowed the man to lecture him. It kept him humble.

Yureni paused before he lifted his gaze to settle on Osuna again. After a few moments, he allowed a hint of a grin to split his face.

"...Didja think I left you because I'm, oh, I don't know, secretly sneaking my stuff back to my cousin's house so I don't move in with you or somethin'?" Yureni asked a moment after Osuna turned away to go and say goodnight to Hemera. His tone was a little teasing, but not so much that he couldn't turn his attitude around if Osuna wasn't in the mood for playfulness. He wrapped his arms around the other's torso from behind and leaned his head on his shoulder. He could see a small smile creep up Osuna's face, so he continued, a wider grin on his own face.

"Or maybe I stole all their stuff and brought it here. I saw you eyeing those pretty rock decorations they've got on the windowsills..." he told Osuna playfully, before giving him an exaggerated kiss on the neck, which Osuna responded to with an unamused swat, hand bonking Yurni in the nose, causing him to chortle.

In past times (meaning two or three days ago, at most), Yureni had shown an odd fondness to Osuna's neck and collarbone, oftentimes peppering them with small kisses for little to no reason. The only explanation he'd ever give was 'I'm fixing the spots without freckles.' Now, he restrained himself from giving Osuna any serious kisses, deciding now would be best for just light teasing, as they were both a little too tired for any real affection. After all, Yureni always tried his hardest to find out what Osuna would prefer at times without directly asking. And, surprisingly, 99% of the time, he knew just what to do.

The 1% resulted in an involuntary slap to the face, on Yureni's part. Osuna had not been in the mood to be frightened that day.

But this was one of the times he was correct in what kind of affection Osuna would like, and Osuna laughed and shoved Yureni off him when Yureni attempted the same action again, shaking his head as he talked in a more hushed voice, as Hemera was probably close to nodding off upstairs. And boy, one did not want to keep Hemera up late.

"Ah, yes, and now I have to run all the way to Priolaine and Fanyu's house and explain to them how they shouldn't beat you to a pulp..." he joked, walking toward the stairs that led to all of their bedrooms. Osuna ceased his movement at the foot of the stairs and turned around, jabbing a finger in Yureni's direction, his eyes slightly creased as he smiled softly.

"Rocks...*pfft*. Enough with these petty little jokes to try and ease my irritation with you, okay? If something out there is so captivating that you make me wait six hours just to make sure you're still alive, I'll have to see it for myself. Maybe next time bring me with you."

Yureni smiled back. Osuna rarely wanted to go on such things with him, but then again, Osuna did always want to spend time outside of the house with others whenever he could. He started to speak up in response to

Osuna's suggestion, but then, all of a sudden, a low voice spread over his mind like a drape.

*He probably doesn't even care for you anyway.*

*Look at how he smiles.*

*He's mocking you.*

Yureni blinked in astonishment at the sudden thought. Sure, he was like any other person his age, he'd had intrusive thoughts darker than the coating of night over the sky, and impulsive ones too, but he'd never have such a thought like that. Was it even a thought? It sounded more like an intrusion into his very soul. Yureni's smile faded, and Osuna, ever perceptive, tilted his head and spoke softly.

"…Yureni, dear? Are you all right?"

Yureni snapped out of the small little slump of discomfiture and trepidation as quickly as it started, and he laughed audibly, masking the small bit of disquietude that slowly settled on his breast, like a weight, or chains.

"Ugh, yeah, yeah, m'all right. Whew, sorry. I had one of those weird ass funks for a minute." He ruffled and rearranged his front bangs, eventually settling on pushing them back as he took a long breath. "Maybe m'havin' a breakdown," he finished with an unsteady chuckle.

Osuna's curiosity slowly changed to concern, and he stepped back down the few stairs he had climbed, making his way back to Yureni.

"What? Yureni, stop that laughing, it's freaking me out. Start over."

Yureni sighed and nodded, dropping his hand from his hair.

"Right, yeah. Sorry, Osu. I–look," he took one of Osuna's tanned hands in his and looked him in the eyes. "I think m'just real tired and stressed from all this searchin' and stuff, and I just need a rest, is all. I know you've been telling me that same thing since day one, and m'sorry I haven't listened, and now I'm negatively impacting the both of us. M'sorry. I'll do better."

Osuna nodded along with Yureni's words, and when Yureni had finished talking, he let a hesitant grin grace his lips. The little pale scar in the corner of his lips on the left side seeming to curl upwards a bit.

"I understand," he agreed, squeezing Yureni's hand reassuringly as he spoke.

"You're stressed. I'm stressed. We need to rest. We need a break. And we'll do that."

Osuna paused after he spoke, briefly, before his stare turned into a bit of a knowing look, and he released Yureni's grip.

"That also means no more of these theories for a while—hey, yeah, I know, I know. You're passionate about them. They really matter to you, and I don't want to take away your passions from you. But I can't have these theories keep you up all night and away all day. Hemera has been sort of driving me crazy when I have to stay alone with her. I never have any answers to the questions she asks me. I have no idea the kind of things she spews of the sky and of what you and her discuss. And when she's with you, it's far too quiet in the house. I think she needs some space to be a child again, without the constant adventure trips. I don't know, Yureni, everything's just too hard right now, and I just—"

He cut himself off and let out an exhausted sigh, closing his eyes. That's another thing Osuna did. Osuna never wanted to truly bicker; he loathed it. He abominated getting antagonistic. So sometimes, when subjects got tense, he'd just shut down and look stressed. Because he was. He was constantly spent from all of the matters he had to balance. Even if he enjoyed being useful and all that, it was demanding. Yureni felt an icky feeling in his stomach at the exhaustion on Osuna's face. He did love his theories, but that feeling he got when he saw people he loved looking like that because of him was more than enough to overshadow that passion. He reached over to tuck a lock of Osuna's hair behind his ear, then traced his hand down a bit lower to cup his cheek. He gave him a halfhearted smile.

"I know. I'll rest, I promise. No more of my chaos for a while," he assured Osuna, kissing his forehead lightly after he spoke. Osuna let out a breath. It sounded cheered, so the feeling in Yureni's gut subsided as he heard it. At least he'd managed to make Osuna's stress decrease a bit. Osuna gave no thanks in reply, but he did reciprocate his smile, and that was enough for Yureni to tell he was grateful. Osuna let a small chuckle slip past his lips, and shoved Yureni off him as gently as he could while still managing to break their embrace, and gave him a grin as he tapped the banister of the staircase.

"All right, all right. Get to sleep, stupid, and maybe you'll quit acting like you're disoriented. And in the morning, if you really rest, we'll send you off to one of your adventures again."

# The Decision

Corsseussula stands in her empty realm of residence, staring out at the mass of space around her. Everything is quiet here. She can think far better when there is the false comfort of nothing else existing. However, she knows the moment she chooses to leave the realm, she'll be greeted with the unwelcoming sight of her responsibilities. No matter how much she hides, they always catch up to her. The goddess sighs to herself, her mind working as quickly as it can, looking for a solution to her problems in the astral bodies of the stars. She can feel the strain of the universe's delicately woven threads, aching with the burden of suspending such a hefty weight. In this vast tapestry of the cosmos, where the stars glimmer like whispered secrets, Corsseussula watches over the universe with a gentle, but unyielding presence. She sees the beauty in the galaxies, the endless dance of creation, and the delicate interplay of life and death.

Yet, there is a steady darkness creeping into her heart—an unbearable weight she cannot lift. Aethis is unraveling the very fabric of the worlds. His so-called "puppets," beings who should have been born with the spark of life and purpose, are nothing more than marionettes, pulled by invisible strings to fulfill his cruel whims. The universe groans beneath the strain of this sickening distortion, and she can feel the fracture deep in her essence. She knows what she must do. She has to stop Aethis—has to destroy the false world he had conjured and release his victims from their puppet-like existence. But there is a price for defying him.

A cruel, terrible price.

If Laphanae finds out about his mother's death, he could be so devastated that he'll never talk to her again. The thought of her husband leaving her had scared her so badly, she'd complied with this horrible event for years and years. Aethis knew the truth of this act, and he reveled in it. He had kept the secret of her sin locked away, knowing that if ever she stood in his way, he could unleash it. He could reveal her darkest moment to the gods and cast her as a murderer—an unforgivable stain upon her purity.

She had lived for eons, balanced and calm, but this war within her is unlike any she has faced before. On one side, the stars cry out for her to act, to save the universe from Aethis' falsehoods. On the other, her own fear binds her in chains, afraid of the ruin he could bring upon her and the ones she loves if she chooses to defy him.

Every moment, her decision feels like a weight growing heavier on her chest. The stars flicker anxiously, as if pleading for her to choose. But a steady, smooth voice is ever present in the back of her mind.

*Not yet*, it hums, *not yet.*

*That's right.*

There is a mortal. Well, there had been several mortals Aethis had stolen away from the world which Laphanae had so carefully crafted, but this one holds promise. His mind is not so easily penetrated, his body not easily usurped. Though the universe perceives him as weak, like all mortals, he possesses more strength than she'd seen in the others.

He could break the world for her. She wouldn't be going back on anything she'd said. She could just…push things along slightly. Yes, that's it. It has to be. Once he grabs ahold of what is really happening around him, he can undermine it. Aethis's power is nothing over someone who refuses insanity.

If she can aid him closer to one of the puppets, forge a mortal with one of Aethis's creations, then…it can be done. All she needs is to be able to cross into Aethis's realm without him knowing. And the only way for him to not know was if he is too blinded by some kind of success.

…success…

Aethis adores teasing mortals. Playing like a cat and a mouse. She knows eventually, he'll confront the poor man like he had several times before.

She'll have to wait until then to slip into his realm. Though she could overpower him, he could still cause harm to her, or banish her. It was his realm, after all. He had power over her if he could sense her presence. But if she went undetected, she'd have no such problem.

This could work.

Corsseussula's resolve begins to solidify like the crystallizing light of the stars. Her heart, once gripped by fear, finds its rhythm again, steady and true. She can no longer allow the universe to tear itself apart, no matter the cost. It was not just the mortal that depends on her, but every life that hangs in the balance—every being who deserves a world untainted by deception and cruelty. But even as her heart beats proudly with a sense of sureness, it does not lighten. She can defy Aethis, but the consequences of her actions will ripple outward, touching everything she had ever known and loved. She has not yet faced what lies ahead, but she will. She has no choice now. Laphanae may hate her for an eternity, but it's better he knows than have Aethis continue to steal his creations away and kill them off cruelly for his own entertainment. Not telling her husband of this would be much worse than confessing something she had done for his own good. Maybe he will understand. Maybe he won't.

But she can't remain silent if she wants the universe to stay in one piece.

Corsseussula's gaze shifts upward, her eyes lifting toward the endless sky above. For a moment, the universe seems to hold its breath, waiting with her. The stars glitter like distant promises, like tiny sparks of hope in the endless night. It is not enough to merely correct the wrongs she has seen. She has to face the truth, not just of the worlds Aethis had twisted, but of her own past. She calls out softly to the sky, her voice steady and full of determination.

"Laphanae."

She doesn't have to wait long before a thundering voice from above her responds. "Yes, my dear?"

Corsseussula does not falter one bit, not in her words, her actions, or even her emotions. She simply holds her head high and speaks clearly.

"I have something to tell you."

# The Tauntings

Yureni knew better than anyone how much the village epically despised him. Okay, fine, despised was a strong word.

They disagreed with him regularly, about quite literally anything and everything that they possibly could. Sometimes it was just random accusations. Things that they'd blame him for if they were too tired to fight with anyone else. He was basically the town's punching bag. But mostly they protested two specific things: his relation to Osuna and his overbearing joyfulness about his theories and discoveries.

It wasn't that people didn't want him around Osuna at all, or that they thought Osuna was a bad person. In fact, quite the opposite. Osuna was almost considered a darling of the village for always being so gentle and courteous. People of all ages would talk to him. Older women would ask him for tea recipes, older men would ask him for help collecting high fruits. Young ladies and men alike asked for dating and beauty advice.

Teenagers asked for help making their own clothes. Mothers or soon-to-be mothers asked for advice on raising children. (Many people mistook Hemera for Osuna's daughter, and he would always give advice on children anyway as he had raised Hemera himself and felt he could explain the topic well.) Fathers asked for help with planting crops, as well as growing them to be as plentiful as Osuna's. (He gave a share to the rest of the village, saying he always had too much). And children just wanted to be around him. Osuna was always so busy doling out favors and helping others that Yureni didn't know how Osuna was always waiting for him whenever he got home.

So it wasn't that they didn't like Osuna, or that they didn't like to see fellow villagers happy with their jobs, tasks, or beliefs. They accepted all religions, because in their logic, nobody really knew what was above or below them or inside their souls, but…

It's just that they all thought his beliefs were crazy tales woven from madness, and technically he couldn't tell them about his relationship with Osuna, so they liked to jeer at him, telling him he was some kind of intruder in Osuna's house. And no matter how much Yureni hated these rumors, Osuna gave a rule not to disclose any information about their relationship. He'd been confused, so very confused, at that first rule. He could recall the exact conversation he'd had with Osuna on the subject while

Osuna and Yureni were tidying up the house a few months back.

"But why, Osu? Are you afraid they'll be cross with you or somethin'?"

"No, Yureni. Do not joke when I tell you to do things for your own good. It's because I don't want them—these people that don't care for you— to have me and Hemera to point in your face. What's going on between you and them is not me or Hemera's business. Do not make it our business."

It was the rare occasion when his partner had been dead serious, and he'd looked it too. It had sent chills down Yureni's spine, remembering how the villagers would say that Osuna had been someone all younger children were afraid of when Osuna was a few years younger. Yureni had brushed it off as an offensive jest until he'd seen how those eyes, those beautiful, doe eyes that were so often filled with care and tranquility, suddenly narrowed into slits of anger and coldness in minutes, and bore holes into his very soul.

He'd never brought it up again.

However, the subject of his beliefs was the main one they all targeted him for. There were a select few (other than Hemera and Osuna) who did not mock him—a newly married couple who'd always greet him kindly, a blind woman well into her forties who would often ask him about how the sky looked that day, or how she looked, or how he was getting along, a few younger children who always wanted to hear his stories, and never complained about them, and a girl of about nineteen and her boyfriend who would ask him daily if he'd found anything new. Then there was everyone else.

As he walked back from a recent trip to try and prove a new theory he'd been pondering for quite a few days, (Hemera had come, but left four days after because it grew boring for her) a young man carrying a basin of water smirked when he glimpsed the telltale red streak amidst bleach-blonde locks.

"What'd ya find Yureni? Lemme guess, some magic berries? Or a fountain of youth? The end of the world? Ooh, no wait, I got it! You found a magic wishing star!"

He tipped his head back and laughed proudly, still carrying the basin.

Yureni's face burned a light shade of pink. Not just out of embarrassment, per se, though it may have been a key factor, but out of the fact that all of what the young man was spewing wasn't even what he was looking for. It wasn't even something he had ever even brought up around other villagers. And it made him irritated that people really thought he was so crazy.

However, he brushed off the snide comments like dust or dirt with a flick of his hair, spilling a few strands of blood-red over his eye and hiked on. His destination was his home for now, where his two cousins lived, Priolaine and Fanyu. He'd be moving out soon to go live with Osuna and Hemera.

He'd never told his cousins about his relationship with Osuna, but by the looks they'd give him when Osuna would call out a greeting to him when they met while passing through the village, they already knew.

As Yureni progressed, a small girl, no older than five, caught his eye. He was perplexed for a second, as he'd never seen her around before, and he'd seen nearly everyone before. Her hair was chestnut brown and tightly curled into what almost looked like springs, and the strands were organized into two space buns atop her head. Her skin was like the bark of a broad pine tree, cheeks flushed red as shiny tears rolled down them shamelessly. She was sniveling over what looked to be a large tear in her dress, which was a simple cotton-white frock that had no sleeves and a faint bloom-skirt-like design towards the end. It was modest, but it looked nice on her. She was barefoot as well, and the dress appeared to be the only thing on her.

Yureni frowned at her tears, pausing in his step. He knew it wouldn't be right to just ignore a crying child, but Yureni usually wasn't the best with children. Well, excluding Hemera, but Hemera was different. She wasn't sensitive and meek, she didn't do cute little things and hide behind her older brother when strangers came by. It was easy to talk to her because she rarely cared about what he said. But a weeping child who was a complete stranger to him could prove to be quite a challenge. But she was no eight-headed monster, surely, so Yureni blew out a breath and reluctantly jogged over to the young girl. She peeked out from under her hands, which had been wiping her sopping eyes in a futile attempt to dry them.

She sniffled at him, before she looked him over and warbled out a question.

"What do you want?"

Yureni debated just walking away, but he forced the thought out of his head and cleared his lungs, folding his hands together as pleasantly as he could, almost attempting to mimic Osuna's usual posture.

"Uh, well, I wanted to ask if you wanted me to help with your dress there. See, m'no professional at sewing or anythin', but I can do a decently good job if it's just simple fabric in a moderately straight line and all—"

"Who even are you?"

Ah, interrupting. This was better, much more like Hemera.

"M'name is Yureni. Uh, I don't know if you've seen me 'round or..."

"Oh- um..."

The girl shifted uncomfortably on her bare feet. She glanced over to the side before she slowly inched further away.

"...Mama probably won't be too mad I ripped my dress, actually," she whispered hesitantly, before she hurried off toward a house on the opposite end of the village.

He cringed inwardly. Oh, how nice, they were telling the children under five now to avoid him. What was next, newborns? Unborn children, even? He could understand them being a little weirded out by him, but there wasn't any reason to hide children from him, or warn them about him.

It's not like he was going to yell at her or even really have a reaction. Why? Well, he'd heard the same words countless times before. And who could blame this young girl anyway? It wouldn't be her fault if that's what she thought of him, her mother had told her so. Just like the mother was told by her friends, who were told by their friend's fiancé, and so on. He was the laughing stock of this place, this whole world. It was his only personality trait according to the majority of the population. He was simply destined for this. He paused and turned around again, walking a little faster to his cousins' house. Hopefully, nobody else would interrupt him.

If they did, however, his cousins would be met with a fountain of colorful mumbling when he arrived back home.

# The First Meeting

*Nothing in this goddamn forest looks different.*

That is the only thought present inside of Aurum's head as he traverses the surrounding clumps of trees, a way off from the village that he has every intention not to return to again. The small clearings between each patch of trees grew smaller and smaller until Aurum found himself among a sea of winding branches and flickering spots of light, melting down onto his face and eyes. If he was in less of a scramble to go home, he would stop to admire how the faint sun highlights the bark of the delicate tree branches so beautifully, giving them a silver hue. Though the beauty of the forest does nothing to ease the tension in his chest and the seeming weight that bears on his ankles and legs, causing him to move slower with every step. He is tired. He hasn't eaten anything at all, and his stomach yowls at him every minute, cramping with a dull ache of pain that makes his situation all the more pathetic.

God, everything is so overly complicated, and he's getting tired of feeling like shit every two seconds. Aurum stops near a tree. Although there are several of the kind within the forest, the tree is rather tall, but not towering, and its leaves are delicate deep-green almond shapes, each layering branch after branch in a wonderful congregation. Nestled tightly in small portions of the dense leaves are large clusters of white flowers, which are accompanied by dark blue, almost black, berries, just waiting, glistening in the radiant rays, edges sparkling brightly, tantalizing. Aurum spares only a glance at the small fruits, however, as he's not quite stupid enough to just grab a handful of the first food he has seen and immediately start stuffing his face. The fruit beckons to him, but he restrains himself and sits down near the trunk, catching a small break before he sets out to continue. As he relaxes, his hands brush over softness, and he looks down to find his hands have met what look at first to be small specks of snow on blades of grasses, but they are flowers instead. Pale, multi-colored flowers, mostly white, are scattered across the area. They hang from long stems in a row, dainty and lovely.

"Look at you, you found the antirrhinums."

Aurum nearly leaps out of his skin at the voice from behind him, and he has to hold back a yelp of surprise, turning around with a confused and shocked look at whomever it was that snuck up on him so easily. A wide pair of silvery bluish grey eyes stares right back at him, and a small smile right below a crooked hooked nose flashes a set of pearly white teeth. There is a mole right next to his right ear, which, like Aurum's, is ever so slightly pointed. All these features are so obvious to Aurum because this person is quite literally forehead to forehead with him. Aurum instinctively smacks the individual in the face, and regrets it instantly as the latter falls back as if they were made of glass. Aurum scrambles back to his feet, hurrying over the person.

"Oh, shit, oh, I'm so sorry, I thought you were going to try and…well, are you going to try and hurt me? I just—"

Aurum stops his frantic spluttering as a peal of laughter cuts sharply through the air, and the person, who Aurum can now see is male, sits up again, shaking his head to fix his messy hair as he chuckles.

"Damn, you know, if I hadn't known you'd be scared, I'd probably be cussin' out your whole bloodline or somethin'. It's fine though, It's fine. I scared you, I deserved that."

Aurum almost laughs along with him. It's quite a contagious laugh, full and hearty and boisterous, as though calling out for others to join in. Aurum returns the man's reply with a faint smile, almost unsure how to respond. Though, before any words can be spoken on his part, his eyes catch the swirl of mahogany atop the man's head, and the familiar glint in his playful orbs. Aurum has to step back to fully comprehend what he is seeing—fact-check it. He takes note of the white cloak, though now lacking the illusion of thinness that water soaked into fabric gave such apparel. Everything is exactly how he recalls it, it's the one thing he's absolutely sure of. Aurum raises a hand to point a finger at the man below him.

"I...know you," He whispers incredulously, mind abuzz with wonder. "My goodness, do I know you! I remember you, yes I do!"

His hands are quaking with the excitement of something finally clicking flooding throughout his entire system. The man on the ground does not share the same state of mind, but he manages a small, hesitant grin, looking to the side slightly before meeting Aurum's gaze.

"Ah, yeah. You're uh..." The man stares blankly at Aurum for a long moment. "Um, I don't know. I don't know you, I'm sorry. Maybe I look like someone else?"

"No, no—" Aurum shakes his head at the man's ridiculous comment. Someone else, his ass. He knows that this is most definitely the man he'd seen earlier, who'd been in that shallow pool. Well, seemingly shallow. It'd been far beyond deep when Aurum had been pulled in.

"You remember me, don't you? I—you were in this tiny pond-water...thing. I'm not sure. It was water, though. Like a small pool. Anyways, you were there, and I was looking into the water, and you grabbed me, and had me pull you halfway out before you yanked me headfirst into it! I remember it clearly!" Aurum says quickly, trying to jog the other's memory as fast as he can, frustrated when he is met with a furrowed brow and a sorry smile.

"…Pond? I'm not fond of swimmin', you know. Makes me feel too weighed down. Doesn't sound like me to be in any little pool of water."

"But I—it was you, it had to be! You have the exact same features and clothes…"

"All right, all right. Say this fellow was me. Okay? What's my name, if you don't mind me askin'?"

Although it's a simple query, Aurum freezes at it. Oh, shit. He'd never bothered to ask the man's name. Well, in his defense, he hadn't had the time to, and it hadn't exactly been his first concern at the time. He gives the man in front of him no form of answer at all, just a simple, dumbfounded glance, at which the man chuckles lightly.

"See? I told you, it wasn't me."

Aurum has no idea what to do. He knows that's not correct at all. It was this man he saw, no doubt about it. Why doesn't he remember him? Aurum chews on the inside of his cheek, thinking back to when he'd encountered this man. He'd pulled him out, fallen in, and woken up dry on the ground…

Aurum blinks.

Dry on the ground. No pool of water beside him at all. That was how he had awoken after he'd been dragged into the depths of the cold water. But that would make no sense at all. Where could the pool have gone? He hadn't been moved, who would just move him? And on top of that, it was impossible for him to have been without a single drop of moisture on him.

"Am I going insane?"

Aurum wonders aloud, voice quiet, mouth drawn into a grim frown. The man's eyebrows raise, but he doesn't look worried.

"No, people make that kind of mistake all the time. You must just be tired or somethin'."

He moves his hands down to one of many pockets on his pants. Aurum hadn't noticed this strange design beforehand, and he watches curiously as the man digs through a few. What is the purpose of having such a large number of pockets? How much space does one man need to carry things?

The man lets out a triumphant "hah!" as he pulls out a fistful of pale purple berries from his left pocket, down near his thigh. He holds them out to the other proudly, expecting Aurum to take some.

"Here, this'll put some sugar into you. Wake you up a little bit, okay?"

Aurum eyes the lavender berries warily, looking back at the man with a pointed gaze.

"You don't expect me to take those. For all I know, this could be some ploy to confuse and then poison me. I will not be fooled by you," he warns, holding up a hand.

The man just looked at him strangely. He shrugs nonchalantly, popping a few of the berries into his waiting mouth.

"Okay, suit yourself," he says, making no move at all to finish his chewing before he speaks.

The action itself ceases Aurum's beliefs that the fruits had a possibility of being poisoned, but he still takes a small amount, and carefully, even though his insides are screaming at him to take more. Small amounts would suffice, even if he was left partially unsatisfied. As the pair eats in silence, a peaceful hush settles over them. Aurum keeps his eyes on the grass below him, examining each and every blade as though it were the most interesting thing he'd ever laid eyes on. What else was there to do?

The man must have decided the silence was too much, as he coughed loudly before sticking out his hand confidently to Aurum.

"Anyway, anyway, my name's Yureni. What's yours?"

Aurum nods, ducking his head in acknowledgement.

"I suppose you'd call me Aurum."

"That's a funny name."

Aurum bites back a retort of "I'm sure Yureni's much more common," as quarreling with a stranger is not something he is any sort of adherent of. Besides, it is true. Aurum has never encountered anyone with the same name, at least, so far. Though, the same could be said for the other. Deciding that a witty response is not a good option, Aurum only agrees with a semblance of a smile, tight-lipped and toothy.

"Right. Uh, so moving on. I don't really know my way around here, but I'm pretty sure that this place we're in now, with all these trees—this must be pretty untouched land?"

Yureni gives a happy nod. "Yep! Nearly untouched, save for myself and a few others, mostly because some have found this place while looking for good fruits from the elder tree." He points upward to the large timber above Aurum's head, the one with the white blossoms. "Or they've just lost their way. But you never really can get lost, I suppose, something' will always be there to help you. A marker of some kind, maybe a smell or sound…something always guides you home, I'll tell you that."

The side of Aurum's mouth lifts up ever so faintly. That sounds nice, the way Yureni is able to describe it.

"Where is your home then? Do you live in the village? I passed by it a while ago, actually. It seemed quaint and simple. I think I may have been malnourished and started seeing things, because I went into a house and got all dizzy and had the oddest dream… I ran out nearly at godspeed. It all looked so run-down and eerie, no offense intended, of course! It looked quite lovely when you—"

Aurum's words slow as he looks up from a particularly long blade of grass he'd been picking at as he spoke and meets Yureni's eyes again.

The man is staring at him, stone-faced, shoulders tensed. He looks almost ready to either throw up or bolt. Aurum stares right back, though his gaze slips a few times as he looks around in puzzlement. What had happened in the span of five seconds? Was there something he missed? Aurum returns his eyes to Yureni, before a sudden shock of worry flashes through him as one possibility crosses his mind. He gets on his knees and snaps his fingers between the other man's eyes, and thank the stars, Yureni blinks.

Aurum breathes an audible sigh of relief. It must have really been a dream earlier then. Yureni gently swats the other's hand away from his face with another playful smirk, but the way it slips a notch does not go unnoticed by Aurum, who frowns.

"What's wrong? You're acting strange all of a sudden."

"That's—how would you know? You don't even know who I am. I'm just surprised, actually. I mean, there's no village around here."

Aurum blinks.

"What?"

"No village. Never seen or heard of one, anyway. Maybe you are really losin' it, friend," Yureni jokes. He gathers the remaining berries, which had been scattered lazily on the ground next to his knee, and shoves them carelessly into the same pocket they had come out of. A bright purple stain smudges the inside of his pocket, but the man either doesn't care or doesn't notice as he shifts to get onto his feet.

Aurum frowns. "I'm sorry if I said anything wrong-"

"No! No, no, no, it's not like that, I'm just…I obviously am not whoever you want to see, so I figured I've already done all I can for you by givin' you some food and all, so I think it's best if I just go home or somethin', so, I hope you find who you're looking for, and stay safe."

Aurum narrows his eyes as Yureni turns to leave, hands in his pockets. No, something's just not adding up.

Aurum quickly rises to his own feet, walking closer to Yureni, who's back is still turned.

"Wait, hang on. Where are you going?"

Yureni raises a brow. "Home," he says, like it's obvious. "I just said I was. You know, like, a place you can sleep with a roof over your head."

"Where's home? You just said you've never heard of the village, but that's the only place I've seen thus far that is a place to stay."

Aurum may be imagining it, but he thinks he sees Yureni's lip twitch and his throat bob after those words are spoken. However, the question goes unanswered, so Aurum presses harder, stepping closer.

"Where is your home then? You said a home is a place with a roof over your head. Where's the roof? Where's the house? It has to be somewhere in the village, so why are you trying to convince me that the village I saw doesn't exist?"

A beat of silence. Neither man moves, and Aurum's words hang in the air. Yureni does not move his gaze off Aurum even for a moment. Then, he abruptly turns and sprints away from the elder tree. Aurum gapes at him. What in the world?

Aurum runs after the man, yelling out, "What is it you have to hide?! Why are you running over something like this?"

No reply, but Aurum was not expecting anything of the sort. Yureni dashes through the shrubbery, eventually slipping through a thick cluster of trees, out of sight. Aurum follows directly, running out through the same opening, sunlight enveloping his face as he emerges from the woods where he'd been encased. Nothing left to block his vision.

But there's nothing to see. Yureni is gone.

Aurum is left breathing deeply, but not panting for breath. Impossible. Where could he have gone?

*You've angered the star.*

*You're a dead man.*

Aurum slams his palm against the side of his skull as if to restart his mind, rid it of those voices. No! God, why won't the voices just go away? This is not what Aurum needs right now. Definitely not. And, what did they know? He hadn't run into any 'star.' Yeah, right. Unless they thought Yureni was a star.

He almost laughs to himself. How stupid. Yeah. Stupid, stupid little voices that keep bothering him for no reason. Not helpful, certainly not of any use. What is even the point they're trying to prove? It's almost like gibberish!

The thoughts almost start to cause his consciousness to ache and he exhales to try and clear his mind. Never mind. It's pointless. These thoughts are only weighing him down, and he can't continue from there. He decides it's better to just go separate ways. He looks to the east. Perhaps eastward is the way to go, he hasn't been there yet.

Just as he is about to head in that direction, his ears pick up the unmistakable sound of a scream.

One Aurum has heard before.
In his nightmares.

# The First Victims

Yureni slammed open the door to the house he and his cousins shared, with a huff.

"I fuckin' hate everyone."

Both his cousins, Priolaine and Fanyu, turned at his words.

Priolaine was a tall young lady, with pale white skin and dark red hair that was cut short at her chin. She was known as one of the beauties of town, though she didn't think so herself, and almost daily there'd be some man at her side, wooed by her tentative nature and soft features. She was typically the calmer of the three, and was very good at stopping fights people started with her, but she was always useless at ending fights between others. Yureni knew that innocence was a cover-up for past times, when she'd been loud—and, quite frankly— annoying. She wanted to erase those years by covering up herself. The loud teenager who'd mud-wrestle Yureni to the ground and tickle him until he'd be gasping for breath seemed like a stranger compared to this current young lady who would look on in horror if other children did such a thing.  Maybe because they reminded her of when she was a child.

Anything that reminded her of her childhood, she'd cut from her life. Even Yureni, in a way. She didn't ignore him, but she did talk to him much less than anyone else, which wasn't much at all because she never really spoke all that much anymore. She'd become so insecure in herself that she barely even talked, barely even moved.

She was miserable.

Fanyu contrasted greatly. He was shorter than Priolaine, at age twenty-two, but still taller than Yureni, and his skin was olive colored. His hair was so long it nearly reached the small of his back, and he wore it in a high ponytail, the strawberry-blonde locks cascading down like a fountain of rose gold. He was the most short-tempered of all of them, but he probably loved them both more than anyone else, even if he sucked at telling them that. His reputation as a protective yet provocative scoundrel also made his name appear in many a conversation amongst the ladies. It was even how his fiancée had discovered him, picking up his name amongst the cluttered gossip that the ladies wove.

Now, however, his eyes were hard like obsidian rock, and they struck into Yureni like poisoned arrows.

Fanyu's eyes narrowed. "This is about those god-awful fantasies, huh?"

Even if they were both only a fraction more discreet and kind about it, both his cousins also believed these theories he was so passionate about were some sort of delusion.

Yureni's head snapped to face Fanyu, glaring at him with a stare of similar intensity.

"I am really not in the mood for this," he grumbled, crossing his arms. "Anyways, they are not fantasies! I've gathered page after page of evidence for you, it took me three whole years to finally get all this information—"

"Information? Of what, that the grass isn't up to your standard or somethin'?"

"—and y'don't even read it and still call me crazy?! You're the one livin' in delusion, Fanyu! Tell him, Priolaine, tell him I'm right!"

"Yureni, listen to yourself, you sound—"

"—Your minds are corrupted, you're not thinkin' outside of the tight little box that others have constricted you inside of! You have no freedom unless you join me, unless we find some way to cut these binding strings!"

Fanyu was looking at him like he was an insect that was getting increasingly difficult to kill, and Priolaine looked blatantly uncomfortable, clasping a wooden plate in her hands that she'd been putting away before Yureni had arrived. She fidgeted with it, tracing her nails along the slightly chipped edges, tracing ridges of imperfections inflected along the years. Fanyu growled yet again, his voice laced with annoyance.

"Fine, whatever you wanna call it. Let's just drop this, I don't wanna start another screamin' match."

Yureni shut his mouth tight, nodding. That at least was something he could agree with. When they got into fights, it was never pretty. Sure, no fights are really appealing, but Yureni and Fanyu's disagreements held a special sort of status in the world of arguments. They were both rather hotheaded, and both knew that well, but they never really tried to change it. Since they loved to call each other out on it, that's what kindled most of their fights. Although at the end of the day, they were still family, and treated each other as such. Both trying to work on themselves without really changing, giving each other half-mumbled apologies and pats on the back, and the next day it would be like they'd never fought. That was just their way.

Priolaine cut through Yureni's inner thoughts by lightly placing a gentle hand on his left arm. He blinked away his previous thoughts and tilted his head.

"Go on, Prio. I'm listenin'."

Priolaine bit her lower lip before she mustered up the courage to talk to the relative she'd lived with for as long as she could remember.

"I think...it's getting late. We should probably start cleaning up the house. I mean—I can just do it if you—"

"We'll help," Yureni finished, nodding.

He knew she would go nowhere with the rest of what she was going to say. Poor Priolaine never was sure of her words. It was as if she were terrified at the very thought that anything she said could be misinterpreted or twisted.

Many people lived in fear of things like the dark, or bad harvest, or losing their loved ones. Priolaine was afraid of any sound that came out of her mouth. Of herself, entirely.

Yureni knew that if she had the decision, she would want to disappear from the world itself. Not that she hated the idea of living, she would just prefer not to be seen, heard, or anything of the sort. Her fear of embarrassment had morphed into a plea to above that she wouldn't be there to make a mistake. Fanyu and Yureni always tried to be easy on her. Getting mad at Priolaine was deeply discouraged, even if nobody had said so out loud. It just seemed too cruel, and her pathetic nature was one that struck a chord of sympathy in almost everyone. And everyone followed this rule to the letter, throughout the whole village.

With that said, all three of them immediately got to work tidying up their house. It was an easy job—their house was rather small for three people—but then again they were very easy to please. Yureni slept on anything solid. Fanyu didn't care what he slept on so long as it didn't try to kill him in his sleep, and Priolaine never objected to anything.

They started with the kitchen. It was the room where they entered the house, so it made more sense to start with what was closer, then they'd move through the house, and finish with the room in which they all slept, so after, they could just go right to sleep. Yureni worked at tidying up the furniture, which was fairly simple. Priolaine worked on cleaning their dishes, soaking a rag into a bucket of fresh water and scrubbing the plates carefully, as she'd already been putting away clean ones earlier. Fanyu worked on sweeping the floors, and making sure anything on the walls was taken care of.

It was silent for a good while. Yureni savored those moments. It wasn't often he was left in silence around his cousins, and he welcomed it. The house being peaceful was nice. However, his happiness at the serene stillness of the room disappeared as Fanyu leaned their broom against the wall with a sigh. Yureni tensed slightly. He knew that kind of sigh.

On everything he loved, if Fanyu was trying to start something…

"Yureni, this has gone far enough."

Yureni whirled around in confusion, looking between them, trying to find an answer. What had he done wrong? Did he arrange the furniture in a weird way that they didn't like?

Priolaine looked over at Fanyu, as if waiting for him to continue. When he didn't, she sighed, set the plate down quietly and carefully, and stepped over to Yureni, next to Fanyu.

"It's regarding, well, your words and actions as of lately," she began, her hands fidgeting as she attempted to get through her point without trailing off in uncertainty and completely denying her opinion on the matter.

"Yureni…the other villagers have been mocking us as well, for this constant behavior you have. And some feel uncomfortable with you talking of your…harsh view of this world around young children. And, this problem was never really any concern to us a few years ago. You know, you were growing up, maturing from being a teenager, and we figured you were just…exploring adulthood and trying to find out what you wanted or believed in…but this has become…a real, actual problem. And it's affecting people around you, not just you, and we think…we have to do something about it."

Her tone was quiet and caring like a gentle breeze, a voice that usually would've made Yureni's shoulders relax and have him just sigh and reiterate what he did earlier, but less assertive.

Usually.

Not this time.

This time her words, her tone, everything, just added fuel to the fire. Because now he felt like she was thinking of him like a rabid animal, only bred to cause problems. Problems. They thought he was a problem. His nails dug into the soft flesh of his own palms, with so much force from his building anger that it was close to drawing blood.

"What?" he asked sharply, eyes gleaming as he processed this new revelation. Fanyu stepped in front of Priolaine and nodded, placing his hands on his hips.

"You've embarrassed us, Yureni—"

"Fanyu, that's a little—"

"Hush, Prio. He preaches of his longing of truth so much. He should be able to handle a little to his face. He should know what people think about him if he's so sure of these little beliefs. After all, it shouldn't affect him since they're the only solution to 'cuttin' the strings'," Fanyu sneered as he stared Yureni down, voice sharp like a carving knife, and mocking. "Cuttin' strings, eh? Hope y'don't mind us cuttin' our ties, then. Don't gimme that goddamn look, Yureni. You've dragged our reputations down the drain with your own. We won't be punished for your actions.

"And I know Osuna's given you a similar lecture on the same thing. He doesn't want to be involved in all of your shit, and neither do we. He's given you a little more grace than we have, but maybe he's easy on you, like he is on everyone. We don't do that. We're not your neighbors or your friends. We're your family, and we're gonna give shit to ya straight. It's for our own good, and maybe one day, you'll learn to understand our situation. I mean, you were gonna move in with Osuna anyway, this is just a little nudge in that direction. Sorry, buddy, we love ya, but we…don't love what you've done to our lives. It's just the hard truth. M'sorry"

Fanyu did not sound sorry in the slightest. Yureni's skin prickled in anger. Yureni had quite the temper himself, even rivaling Fanyu's, but people like Osuna and Priolaine had tamed it for years, to the point where he'd hidden it like Osuna had, but with humor being his relief instead of completely doing a 180 and becoming some kind of wannabe saint. But even so, Fanyu always managed to get under his skin. All that toned down anger had risen up once again, like souls in a graveyard.

"Y'think I'm fuckin' crazy."

Priolaine winced and Fanyu glanced at her briefly, a bit of an apologetic expression passing across his face. Fanyu and Priolaine were close siblings, both of them far closer than either were to Yureni. They were cousins, though, so usually it was easily forgiven. Yureni wasn't worth as much as a sibling to either of them. But he usually understood. He was their cousin, that's the branch he stood firmly on in the family tree. Or at least that's what they'd been told. Yureni never really remembered anyone in his family but his two dear cousins.

Even before Priolaine went all silent, Fanyu had been a very protective older sibling. Protective to the very border of unhealthy sometimes, but he had good intentions. And, well, Priolaine associated Fanyu with her childhood especially, so she shut Fanyu out in a way as well. Not as much as she had Yureni, but it was enough to greatly affect Fanyu. Because of the strain on their relationship as siblings, Fanyu had frantically attempted to fix everything by making sure nothing bad ever happened to her while he was around. Yureni hated it. The only reason Fanyu even cared about this situation was most likely because of some issue Priolaine had. She was a grown adult. It didn't matter if she was embarrassed of a phase she went through, she should get over it already. Yureni was about to make a snide comment on it, but Fanyu nudged Priolaine, and she spoke up tentatively before Yureni could cut in.

"No, no, Yureni, it's not…we just…we aren't responsible for your actions, and we don't want to be held accountable for them."

"You're abandonin' me because y'don't want people to mock you."

Yureni's tone was cold, icy and threatening. Priolaine paled even more than she had originally, when the conversation had started.

Yureni continued. "You don't defend me at all when they mock me, tell me to 'brush it off', but when they start ridiculin' you, it's my fault?"

Yureni could feel small rivers of blood running down his fingers as he dug them further into his palms. He looked up at his cousins, and they both backed away. Priolaine looked at Yureni in fear, and even Fanyu looked a little unsettled. Yureni didn't bother wondering why. He felt a voice snake around his mind and whisper into his ear.

*That's right, Yureni. Show them. Show them the rage you've felt. Show them.*

Yureni took a step closer to Fanyu.

*Hold him. He will not run.*

And he did not. As Yureni grabbed his collar, all Fanyu did was stare. He shouted something, but Yureni heard nothing. All he heard was this voice, this angel, aiding him with his problems. His hands shook and he felt his body go tense. As his vision blurred and hazed, he heard the voice chuckle.

*Now I show you how to cut the strings.*

# The Remains

Aurum doesn't know how, but that scream triggers something inside him, and before he knows it, he is crashing through the silvery orange-tinted leaves that hang from trees like a waterfall. He only has one thought echoing inside of his mind.

*You have to save them*

Who? Oh, Aurum doesn't know. Fool.

He does know, actually. The naive little man knows he understands what needs to be done, but…

Aurum's eyes strain as he continues onward. But he's missing something. A vital part of his memory.

Well, of course he is. He remembers nothing of himself—that has been made obvious nearly a dozen times—but this instance is slightly different.

Aurum can't remember what he knows. It's there, yes, but he can't see it. Why is he running? Did he even hear it? He is running because, something. Something? He doesn't know, he just knows it's something important that's just a little misplaced in his mind. But it's something that he has to find the source of. His head pounds at the thought, the remembrance of the scream echoing in his mind over and over. Ever since Aurum heard that blood curdling cry, his head has been throbbing nonstop. Every thought stings with a burning passion. It hurts to think. It hurts to see. It hurts to do almost everything.

Whoever, whatever made that scream sounded feminine. Everyone probably sounds it when they scream, but Aurum is sure the scream came from the soft lips of a woman. They sounded mortified, and they sounded hurt. It wouldn't be right to ignore it. Maybe it's a ticket out of here? Perhaps it's the start of a nightmare, and it will scare him enough so he'll wake up. Aurum knows that's just fluff in his mind, but it's a sliver of hope, and it makes him run faster. He skids to a stop in front of a house that looks relatively similar to the one Osuna had lived in. However, this one is slate gray, and has an exterior with a few vines snaking up the walls and some delicate white flowers planted right outside of the doorway.

Yes, the scream came from here. Aurum is sure of it. Well not quite sure, but mostly positive. He walks a little closer to the entrance. The door is ajar, and part of the wood is gone. Aurum's blood runs cold with realization. Someone must've broken in. His instincts are telling him to run, but he stays there.

If someone is hurt, he can't just leave them there. But maybe it's a misunderstanding. Maybe they ran into the door and got hurt? Maybe something crashed through the door?

Well it's not certain that there's someone dangerous in there. And if something is not certain, then there is the strong possibility that what Aurum fears is not there at all.

Hopefully.

But hope is a strong emotion.

Aurum peers into the doorway. The whole house is dark, but he can make out two lumps.

Lumps?

There doesn't seem to be anyone here at the moment. That isn't a bad sign, but it is not necessarily a good sign either. If there's nobody here, who made that awful, gut-wrenching scream he had heard?

No, someone has to be here. And if Aurum leaves them that will be cruel and will probably leave a heavy dent in his conscience. If he leaves, it would negatively affect both him and whoever had seemed to be so hurt to cry out so loud that he heard it nearly miles away. And people who are hurt deserve to be helped. Don't they?

Aurum ponders this and then decides.

Yes.

Yes, they do.

Taking his chances and the last of his confidence, he goes in.

Thankfully, nothing springs from the darkness to attack him the moment he peers through the door. There's nothing posing a threat, or not yet anyway. The only thing that's still creeping Aurum out is the fact that there appears to be nobody here, and yet he's certain that the scream came from somewhere inside this place.

Maybe there's something on the ground that can give him a clue of some sort? Great, now it's like a mystery horror story. Aurum hates that type of thing, especially if it's real.

The lumps on the ground spark his curiosity a little. Aurum kneels down on the floor to observe the lumps and is quickly overcome with a sense of heavy dread. People. Motionless, bloodied people. Two of them. There's no doubt about it. As he kneels, the scent of iron, rot, and god knows what else fills his nose. The smell of blood is definitely present, and as Aurum leans forward, it becomes increasingly obvious there is a lingering reek of fecal matter. It's revolting, and it's freaking him out. But there must be someone alive here. Right?

…Well, he has to take risks to reach the end.

The one closest to Aurum is the most bloody and gory, their long ginger tresses splayed out in an array of rose gold, covering their face and neck. The figure appears to be male, from a glance. Aurum inhales and he walks closer to the corpse and braces himself.

It's not enough preparation for what lies in store for him. Aurum is overcome with fear, and the taste of bile fills his throat. He chokes it down, but it rises up again. The strawberry-blonde male—well, what's left of him—

lying still on the floor is dead. His horrid wound makes Aurum's heart rate skyrocket and his breath heavy.

His back is a mess of ripped flesh and poking bones, pillars of fading white and red, still with decaying bits of meat clinging to them. Meat and flesh and bone and blood, arrayed in a gruesome way. A gruesome, yet…fascinating way. Like a colosseum of worthless monuments, flesh gone to waste, returning to the Earth from where it was created. The spilling of red on red, pierced by sharp white thorns, a cage amidst the body.

A cage for the heart that ceased to beat as it once had, silenced by the cold hand of the end.

A bloodstained cage, revealed horribly and brutally in the state of death and rot.

What's left of the skin and insides of his back are a tangled mess of flesh in sickly hues of dark purples and light reds. His organs look like ribbons of squishy material, like browning worms within his body. Aurum almost covers his eyes, and he has to hold his breath to keep from passing out when the flesh—like that of a pomegranate, pink and pale, with an edge of red—becomes more visible as a faint gust of wind blows the man's robes to the side. The skin is raw under the flowing white robes, once elegant, now tarnished and ruined, and blood soaks the floor around them.

Worse, shreds of flesh cover the ground around this unfortunate man, like someone had tried to tear off every layer of his skin, piece by piece, layer by layer. His expression is one of shock, of pain, of pure petrification. His last moments must have been unimaginably excruciating. Aurum can only hope the man died early in whatever process of murder this is.

Aurum's nose burns in both disgust and a feeling of guilt. It runs throughout his body in cold, sickening streams. Why does he feel guilty? This isn't his fault. It can't be. Aurum repeats this over and over to himself, but the feeling of guilt only grows stronger.

Why? Why is the guilt growing like a dandelion at the dawn of spring? Why is he even here? What stops him from running? From escaping?

Aurum shakes his head, grimacing. He has to get a hold of himself. Think, has anyone ever benefited from staying in an endless void-state of 'why'? Asking himself 'why' over and over will only worsen his fear, and will solve none of his problems. Aurum looks over at the other person. Perhaps, they're still alive?

At first glance, Aurum's hopes are diminished. They're most certainly dead.

The other figure's hair is short, about chin-length, and thick, unlike the previous victim's. It is a vibrant shade of red that nearly hides the fact that the hair is matted with blood.

Red on red.

Her neck is at an uncomfortable angle. She must've snapped it, or perhaps gotten strangled. On further observation, a bone is poking out of her neck. It's stained with crimson blood and the way it prods through the pink and light brown of rotting flesh resembles a splintered twig.

Further down her body, Aurum frowns as he realizes he cannot see her shoes or feet poking out from under the hem of her light dress. He creeps over behind her and instantly recoils.

Both of her legs, from below the knee, are gone. Bloodied stumps are concealed beneath a silken dress that blooms crimson where her legs had once been. Her dress, once one of such elegance and beauty, Aurum could guess, one that must have flowed around her body like ocean tides in midsummer, was torn up and dirty, stained in grime and blood. The once pristine silks were nothing but scraps torn into horrific beauty and pain, and the embroidery, the beautiful depictions of suns, moons, and stars that traveled up and down the skirt and bodice like art, was torn out in places or dirtied. The skirt, which must have originally been some shade of white or pale orange or cream, was entirely vermillion now. Her legs must have once been so beautiful, so tall and lean. She must have walked like some sort of empress or noble. Now they are reduced to nothing but the source of a rotting stench in the air that had been assaulting Aurum's senses for the past few minutes.

Aurum shudders and bites his lip to keep from retching. How utterly awful. He feels paralyzed with both fear and uncertainty.

What should he do? There's no saving them, they're both dead. Best to tell someone, he thinks. This incident must have only happened a short while ago, as he had heard someone scream out in agony recently. It's likely nobody knows.

Except...

*Except the one who killed them.*

Aurum wants to slam his head into the wall. Not again.

Aurum steadies his breathing and collects his thoughts. No. He's not going to let these voices get the better of him. He's not going to listen nor bang his head against the wall. Neither will help him right now. He tries to compose himself, telling himself comforting words and suggestions.

No. The voices are wrong. They always are, remember the whole 'you've angered the star' thing? Nobody killed them. Maybe...maybe it was suicide or...

Aurum attempts to comfort himself, but he knows it's futile. Suicide? Who is the boy kidding?

Nobody could have that much damage without dying halfway through the process. There is no serenity, no calm answer. There is only one thing Aurum is sure of.

There is someone-no, not someone. There is something out there that's extremely dangerous. Something that could kill two people and then escape quicker than light itself. And in horror, Aurum realizes it might *still be there*.

# The Third Victim

Yureni ran. And ran.

Never, in all his twenty-two years of life, had he so quickly rushed up that path to the house Osuna and Hemera shared, not even when he'd been hurt or crying or angry. He felt like he was almost missing the ground with each step. Panting and disheveled, every breath he drew felt like some form of torture.

Oh, it was torture.

Sweat beaded at his forehead in salty droplets, and dripped in cold streams down his pale neck muscles, seeming to almost chill his skin. Blood stained his cloak and hands filled the air with the smell of copper and iron. He clutched his hands to his chest, trying to hide it all, trying to forget, trying to convince himself he was dreaming.

He never, ever wanted to look back at that house his cousins lived in ever again.

He didn't even want to go near Osuna's house, so afraid of what he'd done, and if it would happen again.

Priolaine…

Fanyu…

But Osuna as the only one who might know what to do, he was someone who always knew what to do, who to call, what to use… and Yureni needed to find him now. He reached Osuna's door and just threw it open and yelled out at the top of his aching lungs, voice cracking as his face contorted in desperation, those blood-stained teeth poking through dry, cracked lips. They hadn't been cracked before, had they?

"Osuna!"

The man in question was nowhere to be found, and Yureni almost had a panic attack on the floor right then and there. No, no, he needed him. How was he going to fix this, how was he going to find out what was going on and how to fix it? What if he did something again, what if he hurt someone? He needed Osun. Where the hell was he?

Everything was going wrong…everything was too much, too bright, too loud–

"Yureni?"

He froze in the middle of his spiraling and stood bolt upright the moment he heard his name. His eyes, after far too much effort, finally met the thundercloud gray ones below him that were wide with terror. His heart nearly stopped.

Oh fuck.

*Hemera.*

He clenched his jaw and clung onto the doorframe like it was his lifeline. Let go, and all is lost. Cling on, cling on, cling on 'til your skin is withered and your bones decay right before your eyes.

Why her?

Why now?

Oh, god, he didn't know what to say. What was there to say? How would he explain?

Judging from Hemera's blatant stare of distress, of panic, he didn't have much shot at ignoring the thick crimson liquid that seeped and spread through nearly every bit of cloth on his cloak and pants.

He bent down a little at the waist to see eye to eye with her, to reach her level, to try and smile at her, like he used to all the time, but he could tell by her fair skin turning paper-white and her eyes blowing wide, that the expression he's given her was far from a cheerful smile, and judging from the copper taste that had been in his mouth for the past half hour, his teeth were probably showered in blood. There was most likely a little bit of the thick, red liquid leaking out of his lips from the corner. He could picture the image in his mind, and he shuddered a bit, the way his muscles tensed making him feel colder, tighter. But he couldn't help it.

Something was wrong with his body.

He wasn't focused on anything, and his whole form felt heavy and numb. Each time he moved it felt like something else was just pulling and pushing him around.

His mind felt as though it had been sorted through and rearranged, a little bit tossed over to the side, a portion moved to the back, a few chunks added from something else entirely. He felt like a lump of clay being poked and prodded and squeezed into millions of different forms every moment. Colors intensified and then disappeared altogether.

Sometimes he saw three pairs of gray eyes staring at him, and other times he saw none. Everything was either deathly quiet or agonizingly loud. A thousand voices screamed at him from inside of his own skull. It was horrible. Yureni almost wanted to stick his finger in his ear and keep pushing it inside until he reached his brain, and then he'd split the damn thing in half, just so it would *stop*. It was painful to think. The moments when he felt insane were horrid, and the minutes he felt sane were tenfold worse. All of these emotions conflicting in his skull did not bode well for trying to explain himself to the small girl at his feet. He opened his mouth to try and comfort her at the very least, try to ease her growing alarm. However, the voice that was barely even slipping past his lips sounded distorted and raspy, like something else was using him as a ventriloquist dummy.

"Little one…I…I promise you, I—"

"What did you *do*!"

Hemera's high-pitched fearful shriek was loud enough that Yureni winced at her volume, and the tone of pure accusation in her voice.

*No, too loud, Hemera, please, that hurts. I don't want to see black again, the last time I did…*

Yureni reached out to grip her shoulders and felt a pang in his chest when he saw her frantically try to struggle the moment the pads of his fingers made contact with her skin.

*I'm sorry, Hemera. I know I look horrifying. I know I'm scary.*

*Please don't scream. Please don't say anything.*

*Please.*

"Hemera…shh, little one, shh. I… it's…s'okay, I won't—"

"*Get off me!* GET OFF ME!"

Hemera was practically shaking the walls with her cries of pure fear, and Yureni was terrified that someone nearby would hear her. She needed to be quiet for them both, but she wasn't listening to him. She would not stop trying to wriggle her way out of Yureni's arms, tears starting to stain her cheeks and eyes a light pink. Yureni never thought, not once in his life, that he would ever be the cause of the face she was making then. Didn't she trust him? Didn't she remember him? Yureni, the man who was like another sibling to her, who treated her like she was the most special little girl in the whole world? Wasn't he still the same person, even though he was a little dirty?

Though, Yureni knew as he held her that her screams weren't for no reason.

He'd never wished to erase himself before, but one fearful glance from Hemera made him reconsider. She was looking at him as though she was gazing upon a stranger, a madman, an intruder, some kind of psychotic murderer, someone who would do her harm. Oh, how he loathed the look she gave him, he just wanted to see her smile again, he didn't want to see her so shaken, so in fear of him.

Yureni's vision went hazy and the shapes and colors he saw rapidly changed as he wobbled. Although he never even thought it, he felt himself tighten his grip on Hemera.

*No. No.*

*Not her.*

*Anyone but her. Everyone but her, please.*

*You asked for this, child.*

He felt his own control of his limbs go numb and he let out a broken sob. He vaguely heard her scream out in agony as his vision went dark and he squeezed her to his chest.

"I'm sorry, Hemera. I'm so, so sorry."

# The Fake

*So, you run away again, Yureni? How cowardly.*

Aurum squeezes his eyes shut and takes shallow breaths as he sprints away from the home, from the dead people inside, from the blood, from the bile, from everything. It's too much to handle, and the voices inside his skull had only gotten worse the more he stayed there.

The thoughts…they're wrong. Once again, they're wrong, right? They have to be! Aurum is not Yureni, the thoughts aren't meant for him. He realizes how ridiculous that sounds. Thoughts occurring in his own mind aren't his own? Aren't meant for him? He pushes away the possibility that he might be losing it. But then he ponders the thought for a moment.

It may be the best possibility. Probably the best answer, in retrospect. Then all these voices he has heard would be wrong, and that would be a relief. That would mean there was no danger, and, hey, maybe the bodies he saw really were just lumps of fruit or something? If he really is going crazy, then maybe he had just seen things.

Nobody will have died then. Maybe…maybe this whole world is a dream or something! If Aurum is going crazy, then at least this would mean that he is safe at home, even if he's losing it. This brings a note of comfort into his head, and he is content for about three minutes.

Before reality hits.

Aurum almost slaps himself. Is he fucking *serious*? Maybe the malnutrition and sleep deprivation is getting to him. How could he even *think* that going *mental* was *better*? Aurum may not be crazy, but he's certainly on the road to it if he thought it was a good thing. If he truly is going crazy, he needs to get out of wherever the hell this is, and fast.

The trouble is, he doesn't know how, obviously. This world is still a complete mystery to him, unfamiliar and unwelcoming too. His pace begins to slow as he runs out of breath. Aurum can't keep running. For now, that's all he knows. He stops and inhales deeply. The warm air has not changed from when he first arrived here. Strange. Surely there would've been a change in temperature. Aurum regulates his breathing and stares at the horizon. The sun. It hasn't changed one bit. It's still sunset. It's been sunset for hours! Aurum feels a sense of dread settle in his stomach as he realizes it may have even been days. And he hadn't even noticed.

He chides himself silently at missing that major detail. Such important things shouldn't be left unnoticed. He sighs and cranes his neck to gaze at the sun. Something's not right. Something hasn't been right ever since he'd woken up in…wherever this is. A man walks into a house as one man, and then it's like time's been reversed and he's someone else entirely. A man is alive one second, and left as an empty husk the next. And what haunts Aurum the most is what he'd suddenly realized after he'd run away from those mutilated corpses. They looked long rotted. Like they'd been there for quite some time.

And yet.

Aurum had been there to hear someone cry out in pain, probably with their last breath, and the sound had no doubt come from that house. Neither the man nor the woman there had survived, and there was nothing there to insist someone had been injured but escaped. It didn't make any sense. Nothing made any sense. It was like time and space and logic were just being tossed around carelessly like a cat with yarn, like something was playing with his head.

Aurum lets out a defeated exhale, squinting up at the dazzling sun with an ashen expression on his face as he speaks to himself helplessly, trying to make sense of things.

"That can't be right…that would mean no time has passed at all…" "So you've noticed too?"

Aurum whirls around, stunned at the sound of a voice. He recognizes who it is immediately. It's Yureni. He's right next to him, staring at the sun, a happy and content look on his face. His eyes are the same, open and relaxed, ashy blue color prominent against the lighting around them. Aurum is both relieved and scared to see him. How did he sneak up on him like that? Why is he even here?

And...

How did Yureni know Aurum would be here?

At Aurum's silence, Yureni shifts his gaze to him.

"What? Something's wrong? Don't tell me you're going soft on me all of a sudden, buddy."

His tone is as cheerful as his face. Like a bright sunny sky amidst the horrors Aurum had just experienced.

Something is wrong. Very wrong. The sense of dread Aurum has grows stronger, though he's unsure why. It's like the temperature has dropped drastically, even though warm air is still soft on his skin.

Yureni's presence has shifted the atmosphere entirely, and that gives Aurum a sense of unease. So much unease that he finds it hard to form words for a moment. It's as if he's forgotten how to speak. How to think. How to even exist properly.

"Not...Not at all," Aurum stammers, stepping back instinctively.

Yureni raises his eyebrows, unimpressed. He simply shrugs with a grin.

"Oh, just checking."

He hums with a light tone. Aurum can't help it when his lips tug downward.

Yureni's behavior is completely different from the last time they'd seen each other. He doesn't acknowledge anything about running away from Aurum, or the village. Is this some form of gaslighting? A trick? Why would Yureni find him again after running away from him?

"…did…I…Why'd you come back?"

Yureni's smile stays on his face, but an eyebrow raises at Aurum's words. "Huh?"

"You…earlier, you—"

"Earlier?"

"Yes! We talked about the village, and you ran away after I proved you wrong and confronted you!!"

"I've never seen you before in my life."

That statement alone shakes Aurum to his core. No. No, that's impossible. It's only been a few minutes since he last saw him. Wait—no, a few hours?

Aurum's thinking fades as his gaze settles back on Yureni's face. His smile. His smile looks like it's nearly splitting his face in two.

No. No, something is wrong. Something is wrong. This all feels way too weird. Too artificial. Aurum hesitates before speaking again, less to Yureni and more to himself.

"…you don't…look the best, Yureni."

Yureni's head tilts to an uncomfortable angle and he steps closer. "Hm…really? Why? Is something wrong?"

An image in the back of Aurum's mind flickers, but disappears before he can even try to make out what it depicts.

Yureni's smile only widens, as if he can see it as well.

"Ooh, have your chains loosened?"

Before Aurum can even inquire what the actual hell he's going on about, the other's hands shoot out to grab his neck, pressing down on his jugular. Hard. Aurum struggles for breath as Yureni holds him, lifting his form slightly into the air.

The taller man's slender fingers are tight around Aurum's neck, stifling his breath and squeezing the delicate veins. He's looking at Aurum like a cat with a mouse. Teasing him, toying with him. Multicolored stars and splotches of darkness flash and flutter and swim across Aurum's vision as Yureni tightens his hold even more, squeezing the shorter man like a toothpaste bottle. Aurum's blood is rushing to his ears. His lungs are giving out. Everything hurts…every muscle, every bone, hell, he can practically feel every damn nerve in his body sting. It's horrible, suffocating. Aurum attempts to kick him off or fight back against his hold, but he just ends up flailing like a bass caught by a proud fisherman. Even though it's pointless, Aurum perseveres as hard as he can.

*Breathe. Fight. Brea—*

All of a sudden the world around Aurum goes black.

# The Fourth Victim

Yureni was met with the sound of screams. The villagers around him were fleeing, running anywhere but the village. They grabbed hold of relative's or friend's or lover's hands and took off sprinting as if the world itself was crashing down around them. Whispers and yells alike were heard nearly everywhere in the village. The words they spoke were all the same.

"Murderer in the village."

Someone had heard the pleas that Priolaine had used her last breaths to form. Her helpless shrieks, so high pitched they could shatter windows. A neighbor had gone to inspect the home shortly after Yureni had fled. And when they'd seen the remnants of those two, and the blood coating nearly every wall, panic had spread through everyone nearby like a raging wildfire. Of course, they knew immediately who to blame. Even though nobody knew of Yureni's involvement, they all blamed him any-way.

"I always knew he was trouble."

"Filthy sinner."

"He's a maniac. I should've never even let my children near him."

"Mama, he won't try to kill me, will he?!"

Everyone was now running as far from the village as they could, as far as the world allowed them to go.

Anywhere but back.

Anywhere but toward the Winthop's house, toward Yureni, who held Hemera's severed arm in his left hand, blood dripping down his chin and neck, as he stared at the limb with the same look everyone around him wore on their faces.

It was all that had been there when he'd come to. All that was left of her.

All that was left of that sweet, innocent, beautiful little girl who'd tug on his sleeve every minute to get his atten-tion, who used to cling onto his leg when she wanted to play, and giggle uncontrollably when he tried to shake her off. The girl who'd make horrible attempts at flower crowns, the petals and stems wilted and ugly, and force him to wear them along with her all day long while he worked. The girl who he'd whispered goodnights to every evening, the girl he'd always reassure with the fact that she was safe and happy and healthy, wiping shiny crystal tears that leaked out of her eyes as she woke up from nightmares.

Still inside Osuna's house, he simply stared at her arm in silence. No tears spilled, no words of grief were spoken.

He was too horrified to do any of that. What…had he done?

He squeezed the arm tighter and a single tear he hadn't even known was there dripped onto the pink-tinted flesh.

*Hemera.*

*Little Hemera…*

As he sat there, without warning, the door burst open again, and a whoosh of raven hair hurried by, speaking with a tone of urgency and concern that the man scarcely ever used.

"Hemera! We have to leave! The people say they've spotted a—"

Osuna's cry of worry died on his tongue when his eyes locked with Yureni's. With the blood running down his lips. With an arm brandishing the birthmark Hemera had on the back of her wrist. His face almost immediately developed an unreadable expression, and he froze, staring at Yureni.

*"…y-you…didn't…it wasn't…"*

His voice was shaky and uneven, pleading Yureni to tell him what they both knew was reality wasn't true. Begging for this to not be happening.

Begging for Yureni to not have Hemera's blood on his hands.

Yureni dropped the arm and got up quicker than he ever had before, running over to Osuna and grabbing him, much to Osuna's terror. But Yureni did not make any move to hurt him, embracing him in a hug while his voice was laced with heavy relief, though his voice itself sounded like one of a servant of the devil. He sobbed out a few sentences, clutching the other's clothes.

"Oh, thank goodness, darling!! I found you!! I need your hel—"

He was interrupted by a hard shove, sending him a foot or two. He stared at Osuna in stunned disbelief. Did Osuna, Osuna, that kind, beautiful, understanding man who never dared even so much as nudge him on purpose, just push him?

Osuna was not looking at him like he ever had before. His eyebrows couldn't choose between a look of hurt or fury, and they were at a weird position that made him look five times more frightening. His jaw was clenched, and his fists were balled, and he stood with an air of pure rage, one Yureni had only ever seen fractions of, only ever heard rumors of.

Osuna never snapped. He lost patience, sure, but that wasn't anger, that was annoyance. And even his annoyance stemmed from just overall concern, so he'd be gentle with his impatience too.

But never in all of Yureni's life had he seen Osuna so angry.

Yureni had always known that Osuna was nothing but an understanding soul who always saw out both sides of an argument or debate. But it was an unspoken rule that Osuna never was to be bothered about family or friend matters, because he said he despised thinking that any of his loved ones could be the villain in a situation. He hated the idea of them being villains.

And he was staring at Yureni with a look full of hatred.

It didn't matter if he loved Yureni. He could've loved him to the world and back, killed for him, died for him. Sacrificed everything he knew and loved for him, never left his side, always put him before himself.

But.

He hated anyone—it didn't matter who, or even what—who dared to even lay a finger with ill intent on whom he cared about.

Tears were streaming down his cheeks, and he looked angry and hurt. Horrified.

Horrified at what he saw before him, at whom he saw before him. A man he'd loved for years, a man he'd trusted more than anyone else, had broken, shattered every bit of trust Osuna had in less than a second. Yureni wanted to sympathize, I know, I feel it too.

But he didn't feel right saying that when he was being looked at in such a way. Yureni couldn't blame Osuna in the slightest for what he thought, or felt, or did.

Yureni was a murderer now, after all.

"How could you?"

Osuna spoke in a dangerously low voice, his frame shaking as much as his voice as he stared Yureni dead in the eyes.

"How *could you*, Yureni? *How could you?!*"

Too loud. Yureni flinched at the tone before reaching out his hand, trying to snake an arm around his lover, like he'd done for years. When he'd do so in the past, Osuna would laugh and shove him off. He needed that touch right then. He needed to speak. He needed to try and aid his grief, try to explain…

"GET AWAY FROM ME!"

Osuna took a step back, away from Yureni, as if he were some sort of beast. His expression was unlike any he'd ever worn before. The same words Hemera used when she saw him. The same look, too.

Oh…

*No, Osuna, don't give me those eyes.*

Osuna's soft brown-gray eyes were brimming with salty tears, some spilling onto the apples of his cheeks as he stared at Yureni. He looked completely broken, completely defeated, and Yureni's heart ached. Osuna was always so pretty when he cried, soft beads of water pricking at his eyelashes, cheeks slightly flushed pink, shining as the thin streams of water would trickle down them, but this… this was different. This felt like Yureni had just been plunged head-first into a large vat of icy water. Yureni tried to make excuses, speak up to try and explain the voices inside his skull, what they had done to him.

"Osuna…my love, my dear…"

His voice wavered and quaked, nearly fading out entirely as he struggled to piece his words together into some sort of speech. *Stay strong, stay strong. Please let me explain, I would never do this to anyone, I would never...*

"Darling...y'have to listen to me, please...these voices...they told me—they told me I was right, and I could be free..."

"This is no time for your *stupid fucking theories*, Yureni!"

"They said this is our chance. Our one chance. Come with me, please..." Yureni said softly to the man in front of him.

The young boy of seven years, with tears in his eyes and a blackened eye, looking at him like he was some sort of thrilling experience...

The current man, now standing in front of him, tears in his eyes, looking at him as one would look at a roach...

Yureni paused before stepping closer to him, trying again to reach out, trying to touch Osuna, to connect with him once again. To make him listen.

*I could make him listen.*

He waited with a pained expression for Osuna to take his hand, but Osuna slapped his hand away with a look Yureni had never once imagined he could give.

"I would rather die. How could you...how could you do something so horrible?! To my own little sister!! What did she ever do to you?!"

Osuna cried out, loud as a shrieking bird.

*See, he even begs for death. Why deny him his request, Sunset?*

Yureni was trying his best not to hear this voice overlapping Osuna's as he yelled and screamed at him. Everything was too loud again.

But Osuna, his Osuna, would not be harmed tonight.

He cleared his throat, attempting to put on an understanding tone.

"Osuna, please. Listen to me. I– I would never do something like—Hemera. I…I never meant to—"

"You never meant to? Never meant to kill Hemera and EAT HER! I'm not fucking stupid, Yureni! Stop lying to me!"

Osuna cut him off and screamed the last few sentences as if they were for the whole world to hear. As he did, more streams of tears poured down his cheeks. Osuna paused his arguing, breathing hard and shakily, looking at Yureni with disgust. Yureni felt horrible, praying for everything to just be a bad dream. *Please, let me wake up from this nightmare.*

Osuna was staring him down with the look of a broken man. Yureni looked away.

*I don't even deserve to meet his eyes.*

"Osuna, please…listen—"

"Save it! I don't want to hear it!"

Yureni opened his mouth to counter the words spoken so harshly to him, but suddenly that voice, carrying a sense of glee, entered his skull once more.

*Tighten the strings.*

Yureni's hand shot out like a viper and clamped around Osuna's freckled wrist.

NO.

Osuna let out a small hiss of pain as Yureni's skin clashed against his own, and attempted to wriggle out of his tight hold, scowling.

"Hey! Let go of me, what the–"

*Still the strings.*

Yureni's hand twisted in a sharp upwards motion, causing Osuna to cry out as a loud sound of bones cracking and popping filled the air and Osuna's wrist broke.

NO.

He could hear the voice grinning in his mind as his vision faded.

*Cut the strings.*

# The Intersection

Darkness.

For a moment, it's just that.

Emptiness, and nothing but. And then, Aurum can faintly see the shadows of his surroundings. They are quite fuzzy, but slowly, his eyes adjust, and he begins to see distinct figures.

It's Yureni. He's beside Osuna.

Osuna!

Aurum wants to walk up to him, but something stops him. No. He's somehow…not a part of whatever is happening. Only a viewer.

Osuna is yelling and his words come into focus as his face does. Tears are streaming down his cheeks, and he looks angry and hurt. He isn't bleeding or wounded at all, so he seems to be physically fine. Yureni looks scared but also defeated. Aurum squints at him. Although they appear to be so far away, he can just faintly notice Yureni looks a little disheveled. His hair is tangled, his clothes are ripped, and he looks absolutely exhausted, so tired that his eyes looked more gray than blue now.

Yureni must've gotten so disheveled from the forest, he guesses. All that running must've taken some kind of—wait, but Yureni was next to him five seconds ago! Aurum was sure of it. Is this some kind of dream?

Not another dream. This is ridiculous. Aurum is starting to wonder just how many of these he'll have to go through.

Aurum squints at the foggy image, trying to gather some context for what he is seeing. The two men are standing in what looks to be a sort of living room area, with a pot above the fireplace in the corner, the coals below it fizzling out. A large wooden cabinet stands off to the side, and there's a table with three chairs.

It's Osuna's house. No doubt about it. But this doesn't make sense at all. Aurum had assumed Yureni had been denying there being a village because of some sort of knowledge he had that he didn't want Aurum to know, or something he wanted to hide from. But no, Yureni is inside a house in the village, and not just any house. It's Osuna's. What would he even be doing there? Aurum scans over them both, and quickly notices the red coating on Yureni's face, hands, and clothes. His stomach drops.

No wonder Osuna looks so upset. Osuna had seemed to have so much concern for Aurum when he helped him, a stranger in his house. And now, Osuna looks so upset.

Aurum feels a little bad for him. Poor Osuna. Such a worrier.

Wait, but why is he reacting so harshly? Tears seem a bit excessive, and he's not moving to help Yureni in any way, instead only glowering at him. No, something's missing. Something else is going on. Aurum's hearing ability does not improve at all, his eardrums buzzing with frustration at the lack of noise. Not being able to listen for clues of what's going on turns out to be a lot more opposing than Aurum would have guessed. Well, words could be false, and actions can tell far more about someone, so he simply waits for something, some kind of idea of what their situation is.

Osuna yells something out silently, and Yureni cringes slightly in response. Osuna gets no satisfaction from such a reaction, only a faint downturn of his head and a step backward, though Aurum catches a sight of his teeth clenching as limpid teardrops slide down his skin. Before Aurum can gather anything from this, Yureni's hand grabs Osuna's wrist, and he suddenly yanks the man forward.

Aurum's stomach twists just as Osuna's wrist does.

Yureni is a lot of things, and Aurum knows it, but Aurum never once thought of Yureni as dangerous. So, this must be a joke. Or some kind of test? A fever dream? A mirage? What reason would Yureni have to break Osuna's wrist and—

Aurum's thoughts are pierced as he hears a sudden, shrill shriek, the first sound he has heard since the world around him had gone pitch dark. He snaps his attention back in front of him, and immediately wishes he hadn't.

A splatter of red liquid coats the wooden floors, the deep color seeping into the splintery boards, staining them a rich rufescent shade. Aurum's eyes travel upward from the ground, passing shaking legs and firm arms gripping tan skin with an almost animalistic force, to the source of the substance.

The very center of Osuna's chest.

Cloth was ripped aside, the torn edges adorned with slowly crawling blotches of vermillion. Aurum can't see very much of what lies past that, because of Yureni's arm blocking his path of sight, but judging by the blood staining his fingers, especially his nails, and a path steadily dripping a gory river down his chin, Aurum could tell what had happened.

Oh fuck.

Oh *fuck*.

Aurum struggles to remember how to breathe for what feels like forever, and when he finally gets his bearings, he doubles over and screams as loud as he can.

# The Downfall

*Yureni.*

*Yureni, wake up.*

Osuna's voice, no doubt. Echoing through Yureni's ears, soothing his mind like a cold towel on his forehead on a hot day. He let out a long breath and mumbled out a response, his eyelids fluttering. He could vaguely feel cool ground against his skin. He was lying on the floor. That's odd. He has a bed, why had he slept on the floor?

"Osuna," he whispered, his voice nearly silent as he felt his eyes open, but he saw only darkness. He was covered in a warm liquid, and it drenched him from head to toe. He liked this warmth. Osuna must've started the fireplace with the wood he'd chopped for him the other day.

*Yureni.*

He struggled to move, limbs twitching and moving slightly. Why did his legs feel so weighed down? He briefly felt his hand slip on something sticky and squishy.

Probably mud Hemera had tracked in. Silly girl, he'd have to bathe her later. He blinked wearily and rubbed his eyes. He frowned as a red substance got stuck in his eye. It seeped in like thick water, messing up his vision. His sight swam with red-tinged surroundings and sickly ruby lighting.

*Yureni.*

"Osuna."

He mumbled, before his eyes stopped their movement while he'd been trying to remove the substance from his eye. A figure was curled up a few feet away from him, their figure leaking the same red color as the stains on his hands. His breath caught.

*Yureni.*

"…Osuna? OSUNA!"

Yureni didn't know how, but he hurried his heavy legs over to the body in the corner of the room, stumbling down beside it, his face gaunt with a look of absolute horror.

*No.*

*No, this…this isn't…*

He reached out with a shaking hand and found the figure's shoulder, turning them over so he could meet their eyes.

Copper gray met ivory, and Yureni nearly fainted at the sight of Osuna's injuries. No. Injuries was far too tame a word for the wretched sight Yureni's eyes gazed upon.

Osuna's body had been battered and brutalized to the point of un-recognition. Osuna's entire chest looked like it was caved in, the whole thing ripped open in a mess of blood, flesh, and skin tissue. His clothes were completely drenched in his own blood, which was oozing out like a water pump from his chest, emptying every last drop of the scarlet substance onto the hard surface of the floor beneath him, his life essence trickling like sand through an hourglass. Fair and supple bronze skin had paled to a sickly dry-wood color, and veins and arteries were becoming more prominent on his limbs and neck. It was an ugly combination. Blue and purple strings pulsed at his collarbone and at the base of his neck, frantically trying to compensate for the blood lost. A few white ribs stood out like broken pillars of bloodied temples amongst pale pink muscle and skin, all slowly growing redder and redder as the blood continued to move and stain everything it met.

Osuna's hands were clenched around the center of his chest, cinnamon fingers speckled with his own blood. His hands were shaky, and a few veins twitched with blood, attempting to weakly circulate what remained.

He was still alive.

Yureni nearly wept at the fact, but a grim pit of dread in his stomach assured him Osuna's eyes would not keep their gaze much longer. His chest moved up and down so faintly and rarely that Yureni thought he died at least four times. Osuna said nothing, muscles in his throat straining to keep at work as he swallowed hard, trying to gulp up any air left.

Is this how Hemera had looked when she died.

Is this how she felt?

Struggling and helpless, eyes teary, as if begging for death, for a release from the pain. Blood coating every other color with red, slowly succumbing to your fate while you were only half aware of your current state.

Little Hemera, who'd ask questions every time she could, even to herself, just so she was entertained.

Little Hemera who would take the fruits Yureni had gathered with careful hands and immediately try planting ten or so, skin still on them all.

Little Hemera, ever the bright soul, one who everyone would smile upon as she ran by, shouting random words with a broad smile.

Little Hemera who died in his arms.

And her brother, who was about to meet the same fate.

He was so wrapped up in all of this grief and terror that he almost didn't hear when Osuna spoke, his voice hoarse and strained.

"Yureni…you were right."

Yureni's head snapped up at the sound, his face twisting into a look of confusion. "What?" he whispered. His voice was tiny, but he felt even tinier.

Osuna chuckled, but as he did, his breathing worsened and Yureni had to help him push on his chest so he could continue. He didn't even notice the blood seeping onto his fingers. How would he? There were three other innocent people's blood on them.

"…about…the…"

"Don't you say a word about my damn theories, Osuna," Yureni whispered, clutching Osuna's hand tighter.

"…you…"

Osuna inhaled with a painful wheeze and his hands shifted. Yureni's heart sank when he saw what Osuna had been concealing.

Osuna had a gaping hole through his chest. Right where his heart should've been.

Yureni gripped Osuna's hand so hard he thought he might break it. How was Osuna even breathing? Then he remembered.

His body moving jerkily on its own. The odd voices he'd been hearing jeer at him or others around him for weeks. Falling and dreaming and staring at nothing but the blood on his hands.

He hadn't been thinking earlier. He'd been so plagued by his misery and horror and grief, that he'd failed to connect the dots of a vision he himself had created far before this. He was right. His theories, his predictions, everything…it had all been right.

He and Osuna were puppets.

Logic didn't apply to any of them. Neither did any law of physics or medicine. Osuna would die a slow and painful death even without a vital organ. The one word Osuna had said, 'you', hung in his head. He brushed a lock of hair away from Osuna's face as he nodded, tears threatening to spill down his face.

"Yeah, me. I did this. To you. To Hemera. To Priolaine and Fanyu."

"No–"

"Yes."

"No…I meant—"

Osuna let out a breath that sounded more like a choke, and he had to take a long while to pause before he could speak again. His lips tinted darker as a small dewdrop of blood spilled over them. The lips that had sung songs to put Hemera to bed, that had encouraged a neighbor to propose, that he had kissed countless times, that had assured everyone "it is always going to be okay…"

"You…you have to…have to run."

"Run?"

"…yes…the calling, he's *coming*, and he'll…he'll…"

Osuna's urgent tone was hurting his body visibly as he tried to say everything at once, as loud as he could. His body shook like a leaf in the wind and blood poured faster. Yureni couldn't bear the sight.

"Osuna, please. You're dyin', you're seein' things. Don't waste your breath, please."

Osuna's eyes filled with tears of their own. "…I'm sorry."

"No, y'ain't sorry. You shut up right now, idiot. Don't you dare be sorry."

Yureni's voice shook with effort not to cry and break down. He couldn't. He had to at least do one thing right. If he wasn't there for Osuna, he'd fail even more than he already had as a partner. Who was he kidding? he'd already failed so much it probably didn't matter. But he wanted Osuna to leave this world at least a bit satisfied. He didn't want him here alone. Osuna hated that thought, and he knew it. Osuna never admitted it, but he knew his dearest hated being alone. He was always so melancholy when he was alone. So miserable.

He couldn't let Osuna die lonely.

"…Osuna…y'have to promise me when you get up there, you make sure Hemera's okay. You make sure she doesn't harass any of the other villagers, you hear?"

Osuna could only nod, as his eyes grew foggy and he curled up further, trying to stop the blood from spreading.

Yureni hugged him tight.

# The Demon

Aurum is stuck in place. His mind is buzzing with regret, with thoughts. But most of all, with panic. Yureni was right there, standing where Aurum had been what seems like years ago. Is he going to kill him? The images of the two people have faded, and now Aurum only sees darkness. Aurum's head turns feverishly every which way. He's convinced something is just waiting for him in the darkness, waiting for him to turn his back so it can spring out and kill him. Aurum most certainly does not want that to happen. There is nothing he can do, nowhere to go. Fear, anger and sorrow fill his chest, as if he's being weighed down with those emotions. He doesn't know why, but tears spring to his eyes, and soon, he is sobbing. He can't take it anymore.

Aurum wants to go home. He hates it here.

A sudden wave overcomes him. Again? A searing pain shoots through Aurum's head, and he falls onto his knees, hands clawing at his scalp. The pain is unbearable, absolutely unbearable. Aurum feels like he's going to throw up, or pass out, or just die of disturbance or fear. This whole place is horrible, it's so horrible.

Why? Why would he do that? How could Yureni do any of this? He doesn't understand at all how any person could ever do anything so utterly inhumane. He doesn't understand why he still can't look away or close his eyes. The terrible scene is over. Can't the universe leave him alone? It's over!

Luckily for him, the universe seems to have had enough of torturing him.

Aurum comes to, still in what seems to be a black void of empty space, feeling more disoriented than ever before. He stares at his shaky hands that were covering his eyes. His whole body trembles like a birch leaf in heavy October winds. He's so shaken, so scared. He can't control his emotions. Once again, Aurum begins to sob, and not just pitiful, mourning sobs. Terrified, angry, heartbroken sobs that come from the very cavities of his heaving chest. The pathetic child has never felt so alone, so vulnerable. He just wants to go home—wherever home is. He doesn't care if home is hell on Earth. For him, anything is better than this impending madness of knowing nothing, of being a stranger in a world of insanity. He wants to see his family again, if he even has any. His friends. Hell, even people who couldn't care less about him. Whoever they are, wherever they might be. Aurum just knows one thing—now, more than anything, he needs *home.*

Aurum's cries turn into wails. He doesn't care. Nobody's there to hear it, so why should he care? He hopes someone hears it. If they hear it, maybe they'll find him. He begins to get wrapped up in his own thoughts, the feelings pouring out like fountains of misery. The world around him begins to blur, the colors bleeding into one another like a forgotten painting left in the rain. He wonders if he is merely a figment of someone else's dream.

Each breath he takes feels mechanical, as if he is mimicking the actions of life rather than truly living. He has no memory. Maybe that's because he just isn't a real person. Maybe he never even deserved a life at all.

It takes him a while to realize there is a hand on his shoulder, and a voice hushed in a whisper next to him.

*"So you've found the truth, haven't you, star child?"*

The sound of another voice startles Aurum. He takes in a shaky breath and looks beside him. There is a person kneeling there. Their skin is a light, almost glowing color, and their hair hangs down their shoulder in a silky, milky-white braid. Sprouting from their hair are two oaky brown antlers, almost like a deer's. They have a circlet of woven flowers atop their head, and are clothed in bandages and light cloth. The bandages that wrap around their body cover scars tinted a soft pink, and they are scattered over arms like snakes curling over skin. The scars seem to be fairly old, yet they still shine like painful memories.

Their eyes are a soft gray, and they stare at Aurum with mixed emotion. They kind of remind him of an older sort of white bird, like a graceful dove or an elegant swan. Gentle, graceful. And strangely…familiar?

As Aurum looks at this strange Dove-Man, creeping déjà vu envelops him. He has seen them before, he's almost entirely sure. But where? And how? And why is the taste of bile building in the back of his throat in fear? Dove-Man looks at him and smiles gently, with a soft sort of chuckle. It sounds like the noises willow branches make in soft summer evenings. Comforting and almost silent, but beautiful. Aurum sniffles a little at the sound. It comforts him, oddly. And he wants comfort more than anything right now…

*"I'm so proud of you,"* Dove-Man says, his tone light and airy.

Aurum stares at him. In surprise? Fear? Pain? Relief? He doesn't know. He can't tell. Every bit of his body is numb, and he's unsure of everything. Aurum's body doesn't feel like his, it doesn't even feel like a human body anymore. His skin feels like some sort of restrictive cloth, dragging down his soul, and his brain feels like it's been stuffed with cotton. Every thought, every move is a struggle.

Everything feels like too much. Is this even real? Aurum can't tell. He struggles to think correctly, and he isn't sure he can talk. Aurum tries.

No sound comes out of his mouth.

No, no that can't be right. He can talk. He has a voice. He's had a voice for a while. Aurum had a voice before, and he still has it. Right?

"Who…are you?"

The voice that Aurum hears escaping his lips doesn't sound like his. He's all of a sudden unsure of how he spoke. Has he ever spoken before? Dove-Man chuckles good naturedly and sighs a bit.

*"Ah. More like* what *am I, star child. My name is Aethis. I'm the creator and loyal watcher of this world and its people. It's truly a pleasure to finally speak with you face to face. After all, I was getting tired of you playing this silly little game and running around willy-nilly. I'm glad it's finally all out of your system now so we can chat like civilized people."*

Aethis? The name doesn't sit right in Aurum's brain. The creator of this world… Aurum sits up with a start.

"Wait, that would mean that this world isn't—"

*"Real? Or I suppose a better way to describe it is really a false haven. Yes, unfortunately so."*

"And Osuna, and Yureni, and the others…"

*"Are all just living puppets I've placed there. Not real. Never were."*

Aethis flicks his hand and nearly a dozen bodies fall from seemingly nowhere and onto the floor. Aurum yelps at their lifeless faces and severed limbs, before realizing…

They're puppets. All of them. And all of them are exact copies of Yureni, blue-gray eyes open, dull and lifeless. A few severed limbs are thrown here and there, and a few are even missing heads.

The image of Yureni smiling at him like some sort of escaped convict flashes through his head.

Oh. It all makes sense now.

Aurum is frightened now. Terrified, in fact. Aethis has the power to create living things out of what would be considered a simple toy? Is this man a god? Aurum's never heard of power so vast, or so out of the blue. He's trembling slightly with fear or realization. Perhaps both.

Who can tell?

Not him, that's for certain. His brain is far too busy trying to sort out a million other things to care.

"Why am I here?" Aurum asks, his voice strained. It even breaks a little. He feels hot tears start to burn in his eyes. He's confused and in pain in an unfamiliar place. Why wouldn't he cry? Aethis gives the smaller a sympathetic glance, his eyes filled with empathy. No, not empathy.

Almost something like a really bad impression of it. Aethis pauses and then sighs again. *"Oh dear. I've forgotten to say that, haven't I?"*

Silence.

*"It's...quite difficult to explain. You see...ah...you're not exactly...*you. *At the moment."*

Aurum remains quiet. His tongue is numb and heavy in his mouth, like an iron weight. He cannot form words. That's normal, right?

Something deep inside his mind tells him no, but another voice, unlike his own, sweet like dripping honey from a warm pool, purrs in his mind not to dwell on that.

Aurum doesn't know which one to listen to, and now his head is starting to hurt.

*"You must not panic or become angry when I say this. You mustn't be sad. You're another copy of Yureni. Well, no, not quite. You're an experiment I'm working on. I just like to categorize them like this because it's easier to keep track. I like to test my puppets' abilities in this world. Oh, you're not from this world, of course. I've brought you from another. Wiped away some…unnecessary memories to slowly replace them with new ones. You wouldn't have known. You would have lived life just like anyone else."*

Aurum's stomach wrenches and his mind twists with horror as he hears this answer. He prays Aethis is only jesting, just to get some reaction so he can respond with a 'Ha ha, you should've seen your face!' and then whisk Aurum away back home.

But that's probably only ever going to be a fleeting hope.

"What?" Aurum whispers, in disbelief. That can't be possible. It can't.

*"Actually, allow me to reword my previous commentary. You are more of a testing of how exactly I can use my puppets, how much I can have them do and see, what my world is capable of…all of that. I used Yureni's likeness in your mind, because, of course, he was the closest to success. I adjusted your current mind and body out of fractions of Yureni's soul and mind. Like I did with these failures."*

His lip twitches at the pile of crumbling dolls, as if disgusted by them.

*"You'd think that human beings would be more useful with all the talk about them."*

He did not just say that. He did not just say those were former humans.

Aethis is expressionless whilst saying this, and his hair flows as if there is a breeze nearby. But there is no breeze. Barely even any air. There's only darkness.

How can he stay so calm while telling Aurum everything he knows about himself is a lie? Disgust and sorrow fill Aurum's head. He doesn't know whether he should be angry at Aethis or himself or Yureni. Aurum's confusion is slowly becoming desperation. He *needs* to know more. He can't stand this. Aurum forces himself to speak again, his throat croaking as if he hasn't used his voice in years.

"Why?"

Aethis gives a wholehearted smile which makes Aurum's eye twitch inside of its socket. Aurum is absolutely serious. He doesn't have the time for games.

"Why? Why the *fuck* would you kidnap innocent people for your own entertainment, you *monster!*" Aurum screeches at him, blinded by rage in the moment.

Aethis frowns and tilts his head. Aurum has no time to regret his words, no time to apologize or reconsider. A sudden pain blooms in his mind, and he grabs his scalp to keep from falling over headfirst. The pain is awful, unbearable. Aurum looks up at the horned man in front of him, face wretched in agony. Aethis only gives him a mild stare in response.

*"Oh, really? Do you remember that pool of water Yureni was in? You* really *thought the chains inside could stay empty? They needed a hostage and you so graciously volunteered. You freed him from his prison, and in doing so, took his place and are now bound to this world. It is* not *my fault you were bound here. It's your fault, star child. Do not blame* me *for your own foolish actions."*

Aethis says this with distaste, with disgust, as if he is talking to some filthy cockroach, like Aurum is no more than dirt one would walk on.

Insignificant. Weak.

Pointless.

Aurum wants to protest, Aethis's words must be wrong. He opens his mouth to say something but cannot find the words. They're not stringing together properly at all. Words, slippery words, like water running through his fingers.

Water…

Aethis smirks, almost as if he can hear what the lesser is thinking.

*"Oh? You don't think I'm correct?"*

He presses the inside of both of his palms together and then draws an outline of a rectangle in the air. A moment later, the space between him and the air-drawing lessens as a mirror appears right in front of Aurum. Aurum gazes in and does not see his own broken figure on the ground in this strange place.

No.

He sees himself bound in heavy chains, his body limp, eyes closed, as water surrounds his entire form. There are no bubbles escaping his mouth from breath, not even a few. And his head is hung low, hair hiding nearly all of his features.

The pain increases, and Aurum's skull nearly splits in half.

*My fault?*

The strange man insists it was Aurum's fault. He can't seem to remember the man's name. He has one, doesn't he? He's wrong…he must be, right? This can't be Aurum's fault. Right? Funny thing is, Aurum doesn't know why he doesn't believe him. He can't remember a reason why it isn't his fault. Is it his fault?

*Yes.*

Memories flood into the child's mind, memories he has seen before, so very many times.

The man who faded like a flickering candle flame. He told Aurum his name once. Osuna, was that his name? He promptly can't remember. Does he even know him? The man is standing by a large rock, playing a stringed instrument. By the looks of it, a violin. He's very good. The music from the instrument is soft, but the tune is gentle and sweet. Aurum can't look away.

He turns to Aurum and stops playing. A smile is on his face before without notice, it's as if a light switch is flipped off and then back on again. For a moment–just a brief moment–his facial features blur. It's almost like he has no face at all.

And then the scene shifts horribly to the memory Aurum saw mere minutes ago. The man is on the ground, which is stained with varying shades of red. He's not moving, and a large wound that stains his chest like a crack in stone seeps blood onto the ground. Lots of blood. It's almost pouring out of him, like a stream of iron-red liquid. Guilt.

A little girl with bright gray eyes who always messed up her braid. She's walking next to Aurum. Smiling, laughing. Carefree and happy, as children should be.

As she should have been.

And then that same precious, cheerful little girl looks up at him and meets his eyes. The entire atmosphere changes. Her face contorts to a look of horror. She's terrified, and yelling something, but no sound escapes her lips. He can't hear a thing she's saying. Her face grows more desperate, more horrified.

And then she's dead. Lying on the ground, clutching her throat. Her neck is split open and gaping. Her eyes are wide. They look at Aurum with blame and accusation, with fear. A look of utter disgust refuses to hide in her gray irises. He winces, trying to turn his head.

Sorrow.

*Not my fault. Not my fault.*

*My fault?*

*My fault.*

Falling into a void of nothing but empty space, feeling as though icy water were filling his lungs, making it impossible to breathe, to move, to do anything but fall. The sense of dread envelops him for what feels like the millionth time. He knows nothing good lies for him at the bottom of this seemingly endless fall. Why did he jump in? Why did he take the risk?

Regret.

*Why?*

The thought echoes in his mind, cutting through the pain, but not stopping it.

*Why?*

*Why did you leave them? Why didn't you save them? Why didn't you stop yourself? Why did you befriend them just to kill them? Why did you hurt him? Why did you keep going? Why did you kill her? Why did you ever think you deserved to see him? Why did you let yourself be filled with questions and wonders? Why are you alive? Why aren't you dead? Why don't you kill yourself?*

***Why do you deserve to live? Why can't you breathe?***

***You're not even human.***

***So why are you even alive?***

Physical pain clashes with the mental pain he starts to feel. It's not just sorrow and guilt and pain and anger. It's regret. So much regret.

All Aurum can feel is remorse. These memories though not his own, not his pain nor suffering, weigh him down like heavy rocks. Drowning him, sinking him deeper.

Aurum's soul is tied to Yureni's. No, Aurum's soul *is* Yureni's. His memories, his mind, his feelings…they're all Aurum's. It dawns on him as he trembles with the torment he is forced to endure—the voices he's heard. Of course they're not Aurum's thoughts. They're fractions of *Yureni*'s memories and thoughts.

The accusing words, the warnings. It all makes sense now. That would mean that all of these thoughts and visions were caused by Yureni. His life. His warnings. Aurum is too fixated on these ponderings, and in a state of near-shock to acknowledge his pain slowly ebbing away.

Yureni's guilt is what weighs down his body so much. That's why his prison is underwater.

When Aurum does notice the pain dissipate, he stares at Aethis with confused emotions. But it's clear now who Aurum's enemy is. He carefully rises to face him. Aethis gives a small grin at this.

*"Oh dear. Have his memories found you?"*

Aurum nearly shakes with resentment. A nasty sort of evil is all he can see in those pale eyes. Aurum knows he is easily outmatched, but he stands his ground. The fool is not giving up yet. He knows this is the only way he can return back, back to where things are better.

"Yes. They have."

He responds, clenching his fists. His hands seem unnaturally dry. He ignores this.

"And I'm not going to stay here like all your puppets."

Aurum spits out the word 'puppet' like it's a curse. It probably could be, here in this world. He realizes something. Why the world is so beautiful—to mask the horrors behind it. He shakes his head in disgust. This whole situation is sick. Just sick.

Aethis's smile widens at these words and a thrill of excitement dances in his eyes like fire, almost. Fire…nothing more than destruction. Aurum's distaste for him grows ever brighter by the second.

*"You don't get to decide that. All of your guilt will drown your soul. I have killed hundreds of little humans just like you without batting an eye,"* he remarks, folding his hands together, looking almost like an overly-happy sort of nightmare creature. Almost like if an angel were saying this.

He's just like a nightmare. Almost uncannily distant and unbelievable, so much so that he *can't possibly* be real, but horrifying and a threat all the same. His very unreality is what makes him all the more horrifying. The less anyone understands about something, the less real it seems, and the more scary it is. Because really, nobody has any idea what it can and will do. For all Aurum knows, Aethis could be God. Or a close equivalent.

Aethis seems to critique Aurum's silence and then leans down so he's eye level with the smaller. Aurum does not falter. He can't. Aethis beams at that, like he'd been expecting a reaction identical to the one displayed for him.

*"I'm a sort of god who likes games, star child. Games and riddles, puzzles and fun. Like everyone else. I'm simply a sad old gambler, who loves wasting his days for*

*a thrill. I love my wagers, my bets, my stacks of promises. Games with high stakes are my favorite. Everyone's always on the edges of their seats, just craving that next move, starving, thirsting for either a triumphant win or a devastating loss. And yet, the fear only fuels the excitement. Fun, hmm? It's so fun to play, don't you agree?"*

Aethis doesn't laugh, but his grin has spread to what should be an unnaturally large smile, almost seeming like any more would split his face in two. It's a wide and joyful smile, but his eyes…. There is nothing behind that smile. Or those eyes.

Aethis pokes Aurum's cheek playfully, as if he's a close friend, like he's teasing him platonically. Like a buddy. As if he isn't causing Aurum pain if he even *thinks* in a way not to the superior's liking. He's talking to him as if he's a child playing a game of make-believe. Aurum finds this utterly disgusting and wretched. He hates his voice. He despises his games. But right now it's his only option.

The child is going to play these pointless, brutal, stupid, childish little waste of time games. And he is sure he is going to win. Aurum has decided so already, and he is the type of person who makes a decision and sticks with it until they're six feet under. Or, at least, now he's deciding that is who he is.

Aurum is *going* to win. And he's going to make sure of it. "Name it."

Aurum tries to sound as confident as possible. Even overconfident. He wants to put Aethis in his place. He may be a deity, or…whatever he is, but he's also a sick maniac who deserves to rot in the deepest and darkest parts of hell for his actions. And Aurum wants to make sure that happens.

Aethis is grinning from ear to ear now. He stands up straight and folds his hands in front of him. Silence rings in Aurum's ears for a brief moment. Nothing. Absolutely nothing.

And then Aurum sees someone and he jumps back, blood pounding furiously in his chest as his eyes widen.

It's Yureni.

Yureni's eyes are closed, eyelids relaxed. He doesn't even look asleep. He just looks like he's…*there.* He is motionless, bound in chains, hair floating around in the emptiness as if submerged.

Like a puppet without its strings being operated. Limp and ready.

Aurum's lips part with surprise as he lays eyes on the other man. Why would someone else be necessary to have there? No explanation had been given to him at all, which fills his stomach with an unpleasant feeling, sickening and dreadful feeling. Aethis gives a small chortle at the lesser's reaction, covering his mouth with a hand wrapped in thin, silky bandages, almost as pale as his skin. Aethis wraps a hand around Yureni's shoulder gingerly, like a proud inventor showing off his creation, and gives Aurum a look of pride.

*"My, my, star child. You don't look so confident now."*

Aurum tries to give himself some confidence and hope.

This isn't some kind of horror show. Surely.

Maybe.

Hopefully.

Aurum's uncertainty makes him nervous all over again, and that's enough for Aethis to giggle and announce, *"My game is simple. The two puppets cursed with knowledge and curiosity, the strongest I've created, my pride and joys themselves, will fight to the death over freedom, something I've starved you both of for years."*

He gives a howl of laughter and covers his mouth with a hand to try and stop himself.

Goddamn it.

Aurum should've known he'd declare something like this. Of course it'd be something with such brutality and gore as this. Then Aurum freezes and tenses up as he reconsiders what Aethis just said.

Starved of freedom for *years?* Years? Aurum only arrived in this world a few days ago, maybe not even. Time must be funny here. Wait, of course it is, it's always sunset, how could he have noticed the time change? But still, years, he would've surely known if it were that long…right?

Aurum tries to clear his head of those thoughts. Unimportant right now, there are bigger issues. Far bigger. His heart is pumping icy cold rivers of blood through his veins. Aurum is scared, he'll admit. He barely knows

Yureni, and the one time he'd had a proper conversation with the man it hadn't gone wonderfully.

And Aurum is now certain Yureni has murdered innocents. *Brutally.* Aurum's blood pumps feverishly through his veins. Aethis claps his hands together joyfully and Yureni's eyes open. Both his chains and Aurum's drop and clatter onto the ground, the sound echoing like a gong.

*"Let the game begin."*

# The Awakening

400 years.

That's how long he has been underwater.

And for four hundred years, someone has stripped away pieces of his soul, giving others his memories, leaving him with mere scraps. He doesn't know how, but he knows it. He has felt fingers wrap around strings of his essence and pluck them out, one by one, over the centuries. And he knows he's fading, every moment he lives is simply one more moment of painful *unknowing*.

What's your name?

*I have none.*

Who's your family?

*I have none.*

What do you look like?

*Do I even have a body?*

Everything in his mind is unreachable, like it was coated in mist. He has grown used to this and stopped fighting himself years ago.

He is ready to fade out of existence. He can practically feel the tug on his soul. Wait a second.

Those are hands.

He has no time to think before he's yanked from his place under the surface, and his face is hit with a rush of air.

Air.

He hasn't breathed in years, and the light hurts his eyes. Ugh, the sun is always so bright…

After a while of growing accustomed to the light, he realizes the blinding source of such light is not the sun, but a woman.

A huge, towering, glowing, blue-skinned woman with four radiant eyes blinking down at him. He opens his mouth in surprise and stares up at her in silence for a long time before inhaling to speak up, but she holds up her palm to silence him.

"I'm afraid there's no time for questions," She booms out, kneeling down in front of him, eyes scanning his entire figure. A soft smile graces her elegant lips, but it is gone, vanished, the next moment.

"Yureni. You must listen to me."

Yureni? This woman must have the wrong person. He has no name. Not that he can ever remember. How does she know who he is? Sensing his obvious confusion, she repeats herself, more firmly this time.

"No time for questioning," she tells him, before sighing and trying to explain.

"Aethis is trying to kill a human being from Earth. He has no right to do so, yet he has previously, quite a lot. He's taken your soul so he could play around with it and experiment with it in a human's mind. But your soul breaks minds, Yureni, and a human being cannot survive more than a few years with it. You're going to go fight them soon, which is why I'm here to prepare you."

He does not understand. But he nods. If this is important to her, then he will help as best he can. She smiles before reaching into a bunch of silk amidst her radiant, rippling robes, and hands a small stick to him. He simply stares at it and back at her. She chuckles.

"When you wield it, clasp the center tight. It is for defense." He takes it with a nod of thanks and pockets it.

He always has a pocket to spare.

He wonders why.

The woman then brushes the tip of her pointer finger against his forehead, and he feels something click. Though, it doesn't seem significant to him, the woman nods.

"Aethis will try to use more of your soul during the fight. He'll use this, and that will save both you and the human."

She pauses before she nods, her face returning to its solemn expression, but with a small hint of sympathy and worry in all four of her large, pale blue eyes. She gets up from her kneeling position and gives him a final nod.

"Well. The best of luck, my child. May you succeed."

He gives her as much of a smile as he can muster in such an overwhelming and confusing situation as this, and she returns his attempt of a grin with a warm smile of her own. She speaks again, softer, and with a note of pity.

"Hemera and Osuna will be waiting for you."

Yureni doesn't even get to ponder what she's talking about before he's unexpectedly yanked by an unknown force, plunging into darkness yet again.

# The Battle

A sudden voice interrupts Aurum's thoughts. It's female and deep, with a tone of authority.

*Yureni has forgotten.*

*Aethis made sure of that so he could further manipulate him. The puppet in question lost all memory of killing those innocent people.*

*Until of course, you came along. But now he has forgotten once more. Again, because of you.*

Aurum barely has time to think, let alone react. Yureni stands upright almost immediately at the words and looks around. He looks confused for a moment, as if he's unsure how he's even alive. Aethis chuckles wickedly in a way that makes Aurum's blood boil and disappears like a snuffed out candle flame.

The void they are both in suddenly turns to a whole different scene altogether, mimicking the image of a grassy hill at night. The moon is hidden partially behind a cloud, and the sky is deep blue. The night wraps around their surroundings like a black and blue overcoat of darkness, buttoned up with the burning stars.

The grass sways as the breeze makes it dance. Everything around the hill is shrouded in a thick layer of mist, a hush falling over everything as the mist blankets the ground. Aurum looks all around at his surroundings. It's almost pitch black. The stars are his only witnesses. The moon flickers into view, the light shining on the hill alone, its dull, pale-blue light illuminating Aurum's features. Like a spotlight. How sick.

Yureni seems even more puzzled than Aurum is at the shift in…well, everything around them both, and he instantly trips. Aurum looks at him with doubt. He wouldn't be able to fight him if he had an automatic win power. Aurum has to admit he looks pretty pathetic right now. Yureni gets up instantly without a struggle. The air seems to change a bit, seeming thicker. Aurum frowns. That's certainly something strange. He takes a step away from Yureni as he squares his shoulders and straightens.

His eyes lock onto Aurum's and his expression changes from blank to enraged. "You!" He cries out, pointing directly at the space between Aurum's eyes. Yureni's eyes are wide and feral, his teeth clenched together in pure fury. Aurum is taken aback. Yureni's voice sounds just like his own. It's not distant. It's clear and sounds as a voice should sound. And strangely enough it sounds almost identical to his own. It frightens him even more.

Yureni's eyes seem to darken and he points an accusing finger at him, his eyes wide, expression completely deranged. Aurum's scared for sure now, since Yureni is being so threatening. Aurum can vaguely remember having been educated in the past to know that a good chunk of murders, and serial killers, and such, are especially dangerous because they're completely unexpected—even to themselves. Or they're completely normal, and perform like everyone else around them, just more skilled at whatever freakish craft they possess than others.

Aurum would much prefer someone who was crazy to kill him with some kind of manic grin rather than no expression at all.

Aurum swallows hard.

Oh boy.

"All of this. It's because of *you*, isn't it?"

Aurum opens his mouth to say something but he doesn't get to. Yureni pulls a kind of stick out from a pocket on the side of his trousers and spins it through his fingers for a moment. Why would he have a stick? What was he going to do with a stick? Aurum is no expert on weapons, but a stick doesn't seem like the best weapon choice. Easily broken, not much defense, won't impale smoothly, or bash hard enough. He is extremely puzzled.

Aurum's curiosity doesn't last long.

Without missing a beat, Yureni charges towards him and he sees the twirling stick has become a double-bladed scythe, with what looks like fragments of light as the blades.

And Yureni's going to swing it at him.

*Oh shit.*

Aurum jumps out of his way, but Yureni's arm bangs against Aurum hard, and he winces as he feels a bruise form.

Merely a scratch. The tip of the iceberg. Not the biggest problem at hand when Aurum is up against a heavily armed madman, and he's got no armor, weapons, defense, or hiding places. And rapidly depleting energy…

Aurum turns quickly, anticipating an attack. Yureni is on a knee, but unharmed. His head swiftly whirls to face Aurum, a nasty twitch in his left eye.

Oh, yup. He's mad. Probably furious, judging from his eye twitch and the death stare he's giving Aurum — no, more of like an I'm-going-to-slit-your-throat-and-sip-your-guts-out-from-it-like-a- straw stare rather than a death stare. Now Aurum is a little more frightened than he was before. When people are angry, they have stronger and have greater passion to pursue and conquer. And the things just a touch of passion can do…

Aurum backs up a few feet, uncertain of what to do. He has no weapon, and nothing to defend himself with but his own body. This fight is already so predictable. The only way to live is to dodge. But how long can he keep at that for?

Aurum grits his teeth together. No good. There's no way to live. Yureni gets up quickly and raises his scythe. The moon hangs high in the sky, casting an eerie silver light over them as a tense silence rings.

Nothing.

One breath. Two breaths.

It is frightening and filled with a creeping suspense, but Aurum takes this time to use at his advantage. To observe his opponent.

Yureni grips his scythe tightly, as if he'd used it a hundred times prior. As if the grip is so familiar to him, he knows it anywhere. The weapon gleams dangerously, its blade reflecting the moonlight, an intricate design etched along the shaft. Aurum can see how easily the shaft fits into Yureni's hand. Like the weapon was made for him and him alone.

Aurum is not prepared for Yureni to speak out, voice booming. "We could stop fighting."

His tone is harsh, and his eyes are cold. He doesn't look like he is offering some kind of truce. He looks like he wants Aurum's blood to stain the edge of the cool blade of his scythe.

"Surrender. Surrender and I won't have to kill you. You'll just be registered as a failure. The soul removal process doesn't hurt a bit."

Aurum does not answer the offer immediately, but his initial response is a definite no.

Then he thinks of his own body being torn to bits by this large scythe of Yureni's. He swallows hard, but does not agree. Yureni's eyebrow twitches.

"You will lose. You have no weapons, no strength. You are weak. Why do you choose such foolish false pride over a better option?" he chides Aurum, clutching the weapon tighter.

Aurum's mouth is dry, painfully dry, but he has to say *something*, surely. He forces himself to look into Yureni's thundercloud-gray eyes, and inhales deeply as he begins.

"You don't understand a thing about me. You can talk all you want about your superiority, but I can see everything behind those damn eyes," Aurum replies, his voice steady. "And I understand exactly what you are."

With that, Yureni growls in annoyance, and he lunges forward, the blade of his scythe sweeping through the air with a graceful arc. Aurum side steps, his movements fluid and quick, as if he is a wisp of smoke. He retaliates with a swift kick aimed at Yureni's midsection, but Yureni anticipates the move. He spins, using the momentum of his scythe to block Aurum's blow, the metal ringing out like a bell.

Yureni snarls like some kind of chained dog, frustration seeping into his demeanor. He rushes toward Aurum once more, scythe slicing through the air. The blade grazes the shorter man's shoulder, and Aurum's face twists into a pained expression as a trickle of blood slowly makes its way down his arm. Gritting his teeth so hard he worries he almost breaks a few, he refocuses on his current position, stepping back while gripping his injured shoulder to try and stop the blood. Too late. Red liquid seeps through his pale fingers.

Aurum barely catches a glimpse of Yureni's face, but he sees a slight glimmer in the taller man's eyes. Is he…crying?

Yureni rushes toward him, and Aurum hurriedly avoids his attempted strikes, almost losing a leg when he's caught off guard.

*Schwoof.*

Yureni misses his neck by about a centimeter. Ducking was a good idea. Aurum attempts to grab Yureni's scythe. Aurum takes hold of the cool metal rod but is immediately hit in the thigh by Yureni's grip on the weapon, and he releases his grasp, limping backwards.

The cloth covering Aurum's thigh is ripped, and the wound is deep. It stings like nothing he's ever experienced before, and when he glances down at it, he realizes it's smoking a little.

No way. So it was a type of light then. It burned right through Aurum's flesh. The smell of it sends a wave of nausea through his entire body, and he digs his nails into his palm to try and distract himself from it. Aurum can't back down. His life is on the line. Yureni is staring at Aurum, shaking slightly. He still looks furious.

"Why did you have to make him take them away from me? Why did you say all those horrible things?" Yureni's voice convulses along with his hands.

Aurum can tell he's crying now, as shiny tears trickle down his chin. Yureni grips his weapon like it's all he has left. Like if he lets go he'll die. He staggers towards Aurum, face a mix of resentment, repulsion, and spite.

"I'll kill you. I'll fucking *kill you.*"

Once again, he charges. He's starting to remind Aurum of an angry bull. Aurum glances up as he evades Yureni's attacks, trying to find something that'll help. He's getting worse at this. Won't be long before he's dead if he doesn't do something. All Aurum can see is stars.

Stars.

*Stars.*

The words slam into Aurum, cold and clear.

*So if you hurt my children and they look to the stars above for help, I'm going to come down there and throttle you.*

Aurum snaps back to reality with a jolt. He quickly takes mental note of himself. All right, good. Nothing is severed off. Agh…it doesn't matter anyway…how could he ever win in such an unfair fight?

All of a sudden it hits him. The solution to winning. Of course!

But that's a last resort. It would probably fail, and even if it didn't, he would still be in the midst of a total mess. Right now, he needs to try something else.

Aurum quickly remembers that he is in the midst of a battle and quickly hops away as the scythe misses him by a hair. Yureni grunts in frustration.

"Why?" Aurum shouts, ducking and scurrying behind Yureni to try and strangle him. Aurum doesn't expect an answer, truly, and he doesn't care for one, but he's hoping to create a distraction, if only for a minute.

"Why do you want to kill me?"

"Why wouldn't I?" Yureni shouts in response.

Aurum might be imagining, but he hears Yureni choke back what sounds like tears. Now's his chance! Aurum jumps up a bit and encircles his hands around Yureni's neck, so close, so close—

Aurum feels a hard boot kick him in the left knee and he yelps, forced to let go. His knee makes a cracking sound. Not good. Definitely not good. What the hell are Yureni's boots even made of?!

Now Aurum is almost immobile, and nobody can fight like that unless they can somehow heal themselves. He knows he doesn't have that power, even in a world as bizarre as this one.

Aurum scrambles away from Yureni, on the ground now. He'll admit, he's sure he's doomed. One more hit and Aurum will be unable to move. He just cannot win this. Now his thought of making it has gone from a hope to a dream.

Aurum looks up at Yureni, scared for his life. Yureni is standing above him, arms at his side. He raises his weapon and Aurum clenches his fists. He's going to kill him. Aurum looks right into his eyes. Maybe he'll find something there. A shred of regret, of pity, something that shows some emotion other than rage. Just something. Please let him find *something*.

And he does, surprisingly.

Aurum's hopelessness turns to shock as he realizes something. Yureni's crying. A lot. Violently sobbing. His shoulders shake with sobs, and his nose is pink. And, he looks scared too. Horrified, even. Like he's staring death right in the eye instead of another person who's horribly weaker than him. Yureni looks like he's in terrible agony.

He's staring at Aurum with a desperate gaze. Aurum realizes how much Yureni's hands are shaking as he notices the scythe is trembling violently. Aurum is confused now.

What's going on? Yureni does not move. He opens his mouth and his breath comes out weak, like a fading whisper.

"Go. C'mon, get up. Run."

# The Liberation

Aurum is astounded. Yureni is trying to help him? His confusion doesn't last long, and he immediately does as he's told, barely standing up and backing away with struggle when Yureni slams his weapon onto the ground with what sounds like a cry of pain.

Pain? Why?

Aurum backs away carefully, keeping his legs and arms as far back as he can. Yureni looks up at him, his face still wearing that pleading look from when he told him to run. Why would Yureni tell him to run when he's attacking him?

Something is definitely wrong. Yureni's face almost looks like he's in excruciating pain. What? Why would he be hurting? Aurum is the one being chopped up by his weapon lik a fresh piece of deli meat. Aurum frowns as Yureni lifts up his weapon again.

There's something off about his movements. Strangely jerky and unnatural. Almost like a puppet.

Oh.

Aurum can almost feel his heart drop. He understands now.

Yureni's movements…they aren't his own. They're Aethis's. Aethis's movements with Yureni's body. Aethis's words from Yureni's mouth. That explains the choking noises. Aethis is using Yureni exactly like a puppet.

But really he's not. Yureni isn't just some puppet.

A murky image of the two figures floats to the top of Aurum's mind again. It's like sticking his head in a dirty pond, but he doesn't mind it right now. He hopes it will give him some sort of information, some sort of hope…

Aurum shakes his head as the image of the two figures clears. No. Unimportant.

It's clear who the enemy is now. He looks back to Yureni, who stands, trembling slightly. Aurum feels a pang in his heart as he looks at him. Yureni looks scared. Just as scared as Aurum. It's awful, horrible. Whatever's happening to him, he doesn't seem to be able to control it. He shakes violently, tears slipping down his cheeks like rivers of salty sorrow. He's in pain. A lot of pain.

He may not be an original human, but he is still alive. He had a life, a lover, friends, like any other person. And now he's being used like a puppet, which obviously hurts him beyond what Aurum can imagine. He's being forced to either kill an innocent person by his manipulated movements, or be killed. It's horrible. Absolutely horrid. The more Aurum starts to really understand this, the angrier he gets. He can't let this continue. Risky plan seems like his only available option.

Aurum looks back to Yureni and slides so his attack misses the shorter man by just a skinny strand of hair. Then he starts to run over to the hill near the east of the area. It's a rather tall, grassy hill, and it's quite steep on the side Aurum is currently attempting to scale. But that's all right. That's exactly what the little fool wants.

Aurum can hear Yureni's footsteps rapidly approaching him, getting closer and closer. Aurum clenches his jaw, refusing to look back at Yureni. Aurum can feel the injuries on his shoulder and thigh burn, like his limbs are screaming for him to slow down or stop. But he will not falter. Not one bit. Aurum may be a fool for this, but he's also stubborn, and this is one plan he refuses to scrap, even if it seems hopeless.

Aurum refuses to die. Simple as that.

Eventually, Aurum manages to rush up the side of the hill and onto the peak. The hill itself is probably around maybe thirty or forty feet high, and Aurum swallows as that registers in his mind. It's high, sure. But not enough.

However, it's far too late to do anything else, and Yureni is already halfway up the grassy hill, scythe tucked conveniently behind his back, but his hand reaches back for it as he gets closer to Aurum. Aurum looks down from where he is on the hill at Yureni. The more he waits, the less likely it is he'll have a backup plan if this one fails.

Aurum curses himself for being so stupid.

And then he leaps as high as he can into the open air above where the hill descends. No good. Aurum even feels a little stupid. Gravity pulls him back toward the ground. But it's being shockingly slow. Wow. Another 'mishap' with space and time again, and of course Aethis is going to make it happen exactly at his death. He wants him to feel every second of his death, doesn't he? And Aurum can't do anything about it. Everything's moving too slow and too fast all at once. A million thoughts scatter all across his brain, like mice skittering across the floor. He's going to fall. He failed. That's it.

No.

No he can't.

He's defenseless, completely and entirely defenseless. He'll be killed just like that. Yureni won't have any say in the matter, he'll just skewer Aurum right through the chest, and that will be it. Aurum had one chance. And he blew it.

As he plummets to the earth below, he gazes up at the sky. To the woman above. "Please!"

He screams at those small burning masses in the sky, begging them. Begging her. Why isn't she listening?

"Help me! Please!"

They do nothing in response. No… No he can't just fail. He can't just die. Can he?

*You'll see…*

He glances back at the ground and sees Yureni staring at him. Not like a hawk, not locked in on him so he can stab him through the heart.

Staring with a sense of sureness.

Aurum doesn't know what he's thinking. Perhaps in the last moments of life, one's brain will really do anything to attempt to comfort the rest of the body. Maybe he is just thinking only to think, to attempt to reassure himself that he still has the power to control one thing about his life.

Wait. No.

He can do far more than that.

Sure there was always someone whispering in his ear, but he didn't ever listen to them. The decisions he made were always of his own accord. Aethis never once had any control over him. That's why he gave him such an impossible battle. Aethis couldn't control him. And anything Aethis couldn't control, he was scared of.

Aurum lets a small smile meet his face. He was in control the entire time.

Aurum knows the ground is nearing fast, and he's out of time. He closes his eyes as the wind whips his garment. So this is how he goes out. How he dies.

It's not so bad.

The air is warm and fresh on his face, relaxing and easy. Maybe when he dies, he won't feel his wounds anymore, the wounds that ache and sting so much now. He exhales for what he knows will be the last time.

Aurum is terrified. But what can he do?

A tear forms in his left eye and he gazes up at the fading orbs of light, almost like he is in slow motion. Aurum braces himself for the impact of that burning feeling spearing through his chest.

But it doesn't come. He waits. Is he already dead?

Aurum opens his eyes and is surprised by what meets him as he does. He is standing on soft grass, surrounded by a sunset sky—the world he had awoken in. Everything seems to be frozen in place. It almost takes his breath away. It's truly beautiful, but now that he knows what dark secrets are behind this world, it makes him tear up to see something so incredible with such a horrible story. Perhaps he is dead, maybe the impact isn't what one feels before they die.

And yet, something doesn't seem right. He can feel his breath in his chest, the slight tapping beneath the skin of his neck indicates his blood flow. No, Aurum is very much alive.

But where is he?

Some state of consciousness, maybe. That'd explain how everything seems frozen. But how did he get here? Aurum gazes at the sky.

"Thank you," he says softly, clasping his hands together with gratitude. He doesn't exactly know who he's thanking. But for some reason, that phrase seems to slip so easily from his mouth, and it feels right. Aurum cannot be sure of it, but he thinks he hears a soft sigh of contentment in the wind. That is enough for Aurum. He smiles up at the sky.

He hears a soft noise behind him, and he swivels around slowly. A cloaked figure sits a distance away, back facing him, sobbing. A lock of blonde-white hair pokes out of the hood. And the whimpering voice is a little familiar.

Yureni.

Aurum walks up to him carefully. He truly doesn't know whether to be cautious or not. There's a possibility that Yureni is still dangerous, even though he does seem weakened severely.

He's unaware of Aurum's presence. That might be for the better for now. Aurum steps closer to him, unsure exactly what to think. Yureni seems like he needs consoling, but does he deserve it? Aurum exhales, defeated. Oh well. Yureni doesn't seem too harmful at the moment.

Aurum decides maybe risking something is worth it. He carefully stands beside Yureni and tries to get a good look at him. He's got his head in his hands and his face is a mess of tears. He's muttering to himself, most of it gibberish, some of it just words that sound random. Aurum attempts to listen in a little more. The words become more clear, but it's just him saying the same thing over and over.

"Please…I'm sorry…" Yureni whimpers pitifully.

Aurum kneels next to him, curious at what he's talking about exactly. Well, actually he thinks he does know what Yureni is talking about, who he's talking to, but Aurum is still a bit uncertain. It's useless. Yureni won't look at him while he's quiet. It's like Aurum isn't even there.

Aurum ponders if Yureni even can see him, or if he's somehow invisible to him.

Aurum brushes a lock of Yureni's blonde-white hair aside, mixing it with his one clump of reddish hair near the center of his face. All at once, Yureni jerks up and looks at the shorter man in fear. His eyes are rimmed with red, and tears slip down his cheeks like rivers. He looks broken and defeated, like he's just seen someone get shredded to flesh-flavored cream-of-wheat right in front of his eyes.

"Don't come near me!" he screams, pushing himself away from Aurum, his face one of horror, as if he'd just seen the latter pull out one of his eyes and hand it to him. Aurum can't blame him. Yureni has had worse traumatic experiences than any he'd ever even thought of.

Aurum obeys Yureni's words and backs away a few feet. Yureni stares at him for a moment. Aurum tries to touch his shoulder, to help him, to hurt him, who can tell? He flinches. Aurum stops. This is not the same man who tried to attack Aurum. He can't be. He's fragile and an emotional wreck.

He sees Aurum's expression shift and stares at him for a moment. His face crumples and then he continues to weep.

"I'm such a monster…such a monster…"

Aurum gives him a sympathetic look, even though he's certain he's a murderer. "No you're not."

"I am!" Yureni cries, attempting to wipe his tears away, his face pink with sorrow.

"I don't know what's goin' on! I don't know what my name is, my purpose, anythin'! I just remember I'm someone horrible, someone awful…and all I wanted was to get out of here, to be free of this place…"

He sniffles, and Aurum can practically see the pain in his eyes. He's not the same man. He really isn't a monster. He's a puppet. All his sins, everything that he'd done was the fault of Aethis. All of Yureni's thoughts were fed to him by Aethis.

Aurum comes closer to Yureni and pats his shoulder comfortingly. "It's not your fault, Yureni. Aethis, he—"

"Fuck! Don't say that name again! Oh God no… oh, *God…*" Yureni shouts, clamping his hands over his ears so tight that Aurum almost thinks he's trying to yank them right off his head. Yureni bites his bottom lip and swallows another sob, trembling in place like a leaf in the wind. The very name of the god who manipulated him causes him to break? Oh, perhaps the name was meant to strike fear into the puppet's heart to keep him in line.

The thought pains Aurum. How awful. He can't help but feel bad for him. Yureni never asked for any of this. Aurum wraps his arms around the taller one in a hug. He can feel Yureni's body shake in fear. Yureni is so deeply troubled by all his past memories and deeds, he seems to have almost lost himself entirely. He's scarred himself so horribly he's become another man. Why wouldn't he be? He was being forced out of his will to do all of those things.

It was never his intention to cut out a life of suffering for himself. Never even a thought of his.

Aethis had shaped his future, molded it like a piece of clay. None of Yureni's decisions had been Yureni's. Aethis used him just like a puppet. Nothing more.

A few seconds tick by as they hug, Yureni sobbing on Aurum's shoulder. Aurum knows he can't help it. After a few minutes, Aurum speaks up. He knows what he has to say. There's only one thing he can say.

"You can't undo what you've done, Yureni. But you know how to fix things, right?" Aurum pulls away from him to look him right in the eyes.

Both of them know what Aurum means.

Yureni's life is what allows Aethis's plan to continue. No matter how many times Aethis fails in the future, if Yureni is still alive, he can keep making plans. Because Yureni is the only one of his beloved puppets left, and if that puppet is disposed of...

Yureni stares at the other as the comprehension hits him. He nods after a pause and Aurum takes his hands. He does not flinch, but there is fear in those gravel-colored eyes.

"Come on then."

They both rise slowly, Yureni, reluctantly. Aurum chooses to ignore this. It must not be easy, he knows, but it is what must be done, and both of the young men know that.

Aurum leads him over to the pool of water where he first glimpsed Yureni. Yureni looks at the other like a frightened child for a moment. His eyes are wide and full of tears, and he trembles like a small rabbit, nose twitching. Aurum returns his look with a blank stare. He does not deserve any more sympathy. This action is not one Aurum will sugarcoat. That would just be lying.

"I'm scared," Yureni whispers, barely audible. "I don't want to die."

He clings onto Aurum's hand, like he clings to life. Aurum knows he will never be happy if he stays here. For so long, Yureni has been hanging onto life, turning himself into nothing more than a shadow of himself, like a footprint in fresh snow. An empty shell of a man. Some kind of attempt at recreating a human made for the sole purpose of destruction and gain.

It's the only way to repay for all of this. The only way he can possibly fix things. If he dies, nothing more can happen. There will be no more puppets left.

He lets go of Aurum's hand, before he stops. He reaches his fingers down to one of his light brown boots that reach up to his knees, and pulls an object from a sort of sheath in the side of the left boot. It resembles a stick. He hands it to Aurum. Aurum frowns at it, confused, until he realizes it's the scythe Yureni had used earlier.

Aurum stares at him, and now he's hesitant. "Are you sure?"

Aurum asks him quietly.

"I figured…this is what is best."

Yureni replies, his voice light, but his face sad. He manages a trying smile.

"I dunno who Osuna and Hemera really are, but…this lady said they're waitin' for me. And I don't want them to wait any longer."

His words strike a chord in the shorter man's chest, but he manages a simple nod. Aurum presses down on the center of the stick and the scythe blades spring out. He steadies his grip on it, and as quickly as he can, whirls around and slices the blade right across Yureni's pale throat. Red immediately blossoms a bit below his jugular and trickles down his collarbone in steady streams.

The sun starts to fade into the horizon. It's actually becoming night. Yureni looks back at Aurum. His eyes are wet but he's beaming, his breath shaky. Why is he smiling? Why does he look so…happy? Then it hits Aurum.

He's free. Yureni finally got his wish. "…whoa, I think I finally know how…how…"

Yureni never gets to finish his sentence. His eyes roll back in his head and he collapses into the pool, splashing as the water from the pool collides with his body. His figure disappears.

And suddenly, Aurum is falling along with him. But don't worry.

Because this time, he's going home.

# The Truth

Aurum feels like he's been falling for hours, maybe even days. Nothing feels like it once did anymore, but this seems to be one of the least concerning things he has had to deal with in the time he has existed in the current world. Aurum isn't worried about his current situation of what seems like endless falling. He's much more worried about what waits for him once the falling ceases.

His senses have all been shut off like a switch, unaware of whatever is happening around him. Aurum is almost sure he's dead for a few seconds. Then, all of a sudden, he stops falling.

He doesn't hit solid ground, or water, or anything reallyly. He isn't even kneeling or sitting or standing on the ground. He's just suspended in mid-air, as if an invisible force had caught him right before he landed. Aurum hangs limply in the air like a rag doll for a moment, before he feels a tug on his clothes. All of a sudden, he seems to completely reverse his entire descent, yanked upwards faster than he can even register. Higher, and higher, and higher, until out of the blue, he hears a '*pop!*' noise, before he is thrown into the air and lands hard on a rather lumpy surface. Aurum can see again, and he can feel, and he looks around below him at what he seems to have landed on. All he sees below him is a surface of brown that reminds him a lot of the rich color of walnut wood, which slightly varies in color in different areas around him. He can vaguely glimpse some long rope-like objects under the material, varying from a light blue to a lush purple color. A sudden gasp above Aurum makes him jump, and he immediately snaps his head up to try and see who or what made such a noise in the middle of nowhere. His eyes land on two enormous eyes, dark lavender in color, with a slight edge of gray, and he shrieks, moving back away from them as far as he can. Aurum opens his mouth to yell for help of some kind, before the face that the eyes belong to comes more into view, and a smile forms on the giant face's lips.

"Oh, *finally*! I was getting worried!"

The words coming from the being's throat are loud and Aurum can feel his ears ringing. Aurum is speechless as he stares up at the face that is probably about the length of seven of him. Aurum trails his eyes down the being's face, to their neck, to their whole body, and his eyes are nearly popping out of his skull as he realizes where he is. It turns out, the surface he is standing on is not some kind of weird abnormal other-worldly material, it's the palm of a very, very large hand, belonging to an even larger person.

The person in question appears to be male, but it takes Aurum a bit to figure that out, due to the fact that the main facial features seem androgynous so close up. Eyes can't really tell a gender, anyway. But Aurum soon sees that unlike the rest of the body, the chest this being has is the one thing that is not ginormous, so his best bet is that the being is a man. The large man has unnaturally shiny skin, as though he were made of brass, and his lips are full and curved up in a grin. His eyes are big and intimidating, but they are filled with only curiosity and a hint of excitement, not malice. His skin is flawless, and covering that skin on his body is beautiful golden clothing. His hair, which is short, just a bit over his ears and cropped close to the neckline, with a few stray pieces gracing his forehead, flows from his scalp in beautiful curled ringlets of dark hazelnut, which are held in place by a headpiece that intertwines thin wires, donning his forehead and right in front of his ears with impeccable swirls. His chest is adorned with a cover of the shining metal on his sides, a few inches under his shoulders, and the rest of his chest is bare, except for a piece in the center, held up by a gold ring around his neck. It's just a thin circle of gold, seemingly pressed into his skin in the center of his chest. Aurum gapes at the man above him, unsure what to say. His eyes travel back to the man's body instead of his face, mainly just out of fear, and something catches his eye.

That gold ring in the middle of his chest…

The skin inside that circle is nonexistent. Peering through, Aurum can see that inside of the circle is just a void, except for one thing. Aurum's eyes widen in their sockets, and the being holding him chuckles, causing Aurum's footing to slip a bit.

"Yes, that's exactly what you think it is. Must be rather surreal for you," the large man says softly, smiling down at Aurum warmly. Aurum has no response to give. He is in shock.

This man has the entire Earth inside of his chest.

Aurum can see the planet slowly turn within the darkness, the whites and greens and yellows that litter the surface of the great planet taking his breath away entirely. He's never once seen anything like it. He looks up at the man's face and forces himself to splutter out a question.

"I...who are you? I mean...what are you?" Aurum asks, voice shaking more out of uncertainty than fear.

The man simply smiles back at Aurum's lack of confidence, as though he is completely used to such a situation. He simply answers with a cheerful look on his face. "I can tell you both, actually!"

He reaches out his other hand to tap Aurum on the head with his pointer finger. Aurum is a bit puzzled by this, but he doesn't ask.

"Well, for my name, it's Laphanae. If you don't want to struggle with the pronunciation, just call me Creator. As for what I am, I'm the being, the god, really, who created you, and all your friends and family, and everyone else on Earth," he declares proudly.

Aurum blinks in surprise. "So, you know who I am?"

"Of course! I know all about you, Mikah."

Aurum frowns and looks behind him for a moment. Nothing. He looks back at Laphanae's eyes to see them locked right on his figure, and he holds up a hand to correct him.

"There's no—"

"I'm talking to you," the Creator says simply, stopping his words. He chuckles.

"Your name is not Aurum, dear child, I assure you. I knew your name far before you did, and Aurum was never something someone from your home ever once called you."

Laphanae's voice and eyes are still kind and refreshing, but as he speaks the next sentence, there is a tinge of…something less than ecstasy in his tone.

"Aethis and his cryptic names. Whoever names such a creature after *the dawn* just to fit their messed up scenarios? Honestly…But, that's pointless now. I assure you, your name is not Aurum, dear. The name you were given when you arrived into the world as a baby is Mikah. Mikah Krause."

There is a long moment of profound silence, and then the smaller being before the god speaks in a whisper, so small that Laphanae has to lean his enormous face closer to be able to pick up the words spoken.

"Say it again."

The smaller nearly begs, clasping his hands together as though he is a sinner in the presence of a priest, pleading up at the god with those stone-gray eyes. Laphanae asks no questions. He already knows the reasoning behind the request. He smiles down at the man.

"Your name is Mikah Krause," he repeats, his voice soothing and gentle. He knows such a topic can be delicate. Mikah has no idea who he is.

Mikah lets out a small whimper, falling onto his knees, head in his hands, just sitting there. The god before him does not comment on the action. He only waits for a response, patient and silent.

Mikah cannot comprehend his own name. His thoughts are filled with that same word, that beautiful word.

*Mikah. My name is Mikah.*

Mikah looks back up at Laphanae slowly, peeking out from his hands that shield his face. His voice wobbles when he speaks, almost as if he really were some kind of naive child.

"I apologize for asking so much from you, but if you could, please, tell me more. I need to know who I am."

"No, not to worry, dear, all your memories will be restored once I figure out how to remove the ones implanted inside your soul that are blocking the—"

"No!"

Mikah says it so fast, he almost doesn't realize he's interrupted the deity until Laphanae stops and just stares blankly at him, quirking an eyebrow. Mikah's face quickly flushes a ruby red hue, and he bites his lower lip out of embarrassment. He just interrupted a god who's probably three hundred times his size, and could crush the mortal right there in his palm if he saw fit. Mikah remembers who he is talking to, and he quickly holds up his hands in defense.

"Sorry, sorry. I'm sorry. I didn't mean anything offensive by that, or that I don't want my memories back…"

Mikah attempts to redeem himself, talking sheepishly the whole time. He can't decide if he wants to avoid Laphanae's gaze, or stare him right in the eye. Though, it is a bit hard for him not to stare him dead in the eye, as the deity's eyes are probably the same size as Mikah's whole body from head to toe. All Mikah can really focus on are those deep purple irises as he musters up any answer he can before getting to his actual reasoning for the sudden interruption.

"I just…could you please at least give me a little background? It can be any time you want to tell me, just before you give me back all my memories—"

Before the god even registers all the words coming out of his mouth, Mikah cuts himself off and raises his voice with a turn of slight urgency.

"Wait, what will I even do with those memories? I can't go home, I'm st—"

"You can very well return home, dear," Laphane insists gently, nodding so his dark curls bounce ever so slightly on his head.

His regal headpiece clinks as his chin moves. Mikah stares at him in awe. The god is just so…calm. Unbothered, even. With fair reason, he probably knows everything there is to know about the universe and its ways. And, he quite literally has the entire planet of Earth inside of his chest. If Mikah can trust anyone on such a topic, most likely it is the god currently with him. Mikah swallows down his fear, but it still lodges tight in his throat, even as he is reassured.

"I can?" he asks Laphanae, perking up a bit from his place, cupped in the god's hand.

He'd figured that there'd be some kind of divine tie of his soul to Aethis's world, and Laphnae, although he looks more than powerful, may not be allowed to intervene. Then again, Mikah has technically won the game Aethis had laid out for him, which does mean he is entitled to his freedom. It slowly starts to make more sense to him as to why he can return home.

Laphanae must be able to see the apprehension on the little one's face, because he lets out an amused hum and nods.

"Indeed, you can. It is as simple as blinking, dear, I assure you. You need not worry about your return."

Laphanae gives Mikah a final grin, his hands lifting the smaller man higher.

"Now, kneel," the god orders him quietly.

Mikah nods obediently, shifting his position so he is holding himself up by the knees. He bows his head as the god tilts his head closer. Mikah doesn't know why such a gesture feels so right. But it does not feel wrong, so he stays there, long white strands of hair covering his face as he remains kneeling.

"You will feel as though you are falling," Laphanae admits, giggling slightly as he talks. "But I am sure you are no stranger to such a sensation by now."

Mikah does not have any time to give the god a reply, but even if he had the chance, he would have chosen not to speak. Although the god has not wronged him in any way, unlike a certain braid-wearing one he had met before, Mikah would prefer to leave this odd place of gods and puppets as soon as possible without any more interactions. He hopes Laphanae will understand, which the deity probably will. Such a kind creature must be an empathetic one as well.

Mikah will not miss this world, no matter how many inhuman beings save him, but he will remember the actions of such creatures for years to come.

Mikah closes his eyes as his limbs begin to tingle, the feeling turning into a disturbing numbness as it spreads from the tips of his fingers to the rest of his body, completely enveloping him in a feeling of simply existing as nothing. Though now, the feeling does not scare or plague him. In fact, it now feels like a sense of relaxation.

Finally, he is nothing. Which means soon, he will be something, something he knows, something he can exist as, knowing he exists, knowing he's real, and he's alive.

Mikah lets his eyes open as his body goes from feeling like it is floating in a void to being dropped from the air. His long hair whips around his face, tickling his ears and cheeks as he falls. Slowly, however, the lengthy, oddly chopped layers of pale hair start to shorten, as if receding back to his skull. White locks turn a shade of brown that almost looks black. His hair goes from being down to his waist to just cut a bit below his ears, with a good amount of length in the back. Mikah's eyes widen as he watches himself change right before his own eyes. As he watches his skin grow a natural flush that just feels so *normal* and *real*, he can practically see the words in his mind.

*Name: Mikah Krause*

His eyes go from a near-lifeless shade of gray to a soft, hazel color, his eyes going from big and doll-like to a more droopy and realistic kind. No perfect skin, he has a faint shadow under each eye, and his pink lips pale to a more natural color. They feel dry and cracked, but Mikah's never felt more perfect lips on his body. Those lips…

He knows. He knows exactly what his face has experienced through the years. He can remember a tall woman with black hair stroking the hair on his head as he lay on his bed as a child. A boy around fourteen poking him on the nose with a wide grin as he points to the snow outside. A girl, now around his age, mouthing something he can't hear.

And then she kisses him. She tastes sweet.

*Age: 20 years old*

The cloaks and silks made of that white and cream-colored material fade instantly, and give way to a pair of dark gray sweatpants and a white turtleneck with sleeves that stop right before his shoulder meets the path to his elbow. The length of the top reveals a few line-straight scars on both of his wrists, which are quickly covered by some Band-Aids. Mikah can remember. He can remember the exact time he got every single one.

Standing over the bathtub with a razor in his hands. A man walks in and takes it from his fingers, and hugs him tight. Mikah can remember how the moment felt. Silent. He could remember after the fact as well. A phone call with three other people on it, laughing and smiling. A girl with pin-straight red hair nodding at him with a kind smile as if he's speaking to her.

And that same girl he'd kissed, pressing little Hello-Kitty Band-Aids onto every single cut.

She's looking up at him and grinning, and she puts one over his nose just for fun.

Mikah closes his eyes and his thin lips turn upwards into a smile as the memories fill his head.

*Home: Found*

# The Aftermath I

"NO!"

The unmistakable sound of frustrated yelling and rage absolutely encases the entirety of Aethis's realm. The flowers wither. The grass shrivels. The breeze turns to a cold wind as he paces, his eyes wide and boggling, his braid whipping in the wind. He looks absolutely enraged as he walks, eyes nearly popping out of his sockets, hair in his braid starting to come loose, and face completely contorted into something nearly impossible with anger as he moves in the same circles over and over.

"HOW COULD THIS HAVE HAPPENED? I PLANNED IT ALL OUT PERFECTLY!"

Aethis has gone mad. Drunk on rage and self-loathing for failure, because, truly, how had he failed?

There had been absolutely no possibility of either of those filthy brats finding peace, leaving this world. He had perfected this plan for billions of years. The moment he'd discovered his true capabilities, his intelligence compared to others around him, he'd formulated this very plan, checked and proofed it, made sure every single possibility, every single aspect, was nothing less than absolute perfection. He'd taken his time, too. Each step was thought out like a beautiful, delicate, piece of art. Not a thing was rushed or dragged on. He aligned everything with such precision that it was impossible to even suggest failure. To even think of it. Because truly, he had taken every precaution. Nothing was supposed to have gone wrong. Nothing could have gone wrong.

So *how?*

In the midst of all his ranting, his ears pick up the familiar sound of a light chuckle.

He immediately whips his head in the direction of the giggle.

Giggling? At him? Mocking him?

He turns in fury, only to be met with fair blue robes that shift as the person beside him changes their posture upon being gazed at. He moves his gaze upward to see two pairs of milky white eyes with long gray-blue eyelashes that fold over her lids like curtains of solid water, like ice — her, that god awful woman of stars that had promised him that these puppets were, well, puppets! Puppets with no minds of their own, puppets that wouldn't take off with a human, develop a consciousness that no matter how hard he tried, he couldn't fully possess for more than an hour, and then abruptly die and take everyone else with them!

They were supposed to be brainless, oblivious! This liar! He suddenly snaps as a vein throbs in his temple, and he starts yelling once more, jamming an accusing finger at her face.

"We made a deal, Corsseussula! A deal. You wench. You horrible schemer! You lied to me! You thought of me as a fool!"

"I mean, aren't you, if you believed I would actually let you interfere with Laphanae's creations?"

Corsseussula's face is a dismissive one, as if she thinks Aethis must be truly idiotic to think such things. Although Aethis' intelligence rivals many of the wings around him, it could never compare to her own. She had shaped the very universe, shaped the beings who'd brought *him* into existence. Of course she could interpret a silly little scheme of his and foil it. It was truly too easy for the goddess. Her face is one of an unbothered elder who's instructing a lesser, but as she gets around to the topic of humanity and Laphanae, her face hardens into a furious scowl. All four of her beautiful eyes widen in anger.

"You made Laphanae feel like a *failure*. Don't you know how hard he works? How much he tries to make the world a good place for his children? How he keeps the balance as well as he possibly can? And you ruined the bond of peace the universe has. You caused universe-wide problems, problems that will require centuries to repair, and I'm the one at fault here? You are such a *child*. It's pathetic, truly."

She scolds with anger that runs cold, like ice in her veins. Silent, but equally as deadly as the flames of Aethis's anger, which run hot, if not more so. Aethis, however, merely snorts at her comment, as if unaffected by what he has done to humanity and to Laphanae's self-esteem. Perhaps even amused.

"I couldn't care less about Laphanae's feelings. He's a grown man, and a god at that, not some child. That's exactly why I can't understand you. You coddle him like an infant, trying to shield him from *mean little Aethis?*"

As he talks, all of Corsseussula's muscles tense up, and her pale eyes twitch at every word. She speaks up, her tone one of great warning, carrying nothing but malice and hate.

"Listen to me very carefully, Aethis. One more word that isn't acceptance for what you've done and your punishment…"

"Oh please, like I'm going to be *afraid* of the Goddess of *Stars*. What are you going to do? Refuse to make me a constellation? Ooh, or maybe you and Laphanae can shoot some glowing stars at me? Ooh, I feel so threatened! Please, have mercy."

His sarcasm drips, and it's almost painfully unattractive the way his face wrinkles in sarcasm as he mocks her words.

"I may have had respect for you once, Corsseussula, but that ship has sailed. Destruction ruined me, you took away my position, it is not my fault I am how I am. But now, my power far exceeds yours, and don't forget—we did make a deal. I've got that little detail on Laphanae's dearest late mother, and I'm not afraid to tell him anything. I am not afraid of a little *goddess of stars*."

Her eyebrow quirks and she stares down at the smaller with that same intense stare.

"Who said I was punishing you?"

"I—what?"

Her grin spreads across her face like a cat after cornering a canary.

"I may be fuming with you right now, but I'm always frustrated with you. You know my anger well, so you've developed a tolerance for it. I've never followed through on my threats because unlike you, I care about how my morals align with my actions. Or, just morals in general."

She shrugged.

"That's not the main reason, however. I beat you to it, and told my dear husband myself about his mother's death. He learned the details, discovered that I killed her because of her attempt to end his life, and easily accepted an apology with the only issue being the fact that it was his mother and he would've liked an earlier explanation. Naturally, I then told him everything that had been happening for the past four hundred years, and he cared far more about your interference with the universe than any blackmail you could have against me. Now I ask you, Aethis. Have you ever seen Laphanae angry?"

Aethis's eyes widen in absolute shock.

*No. She wouldn't. Surely, she is bluffing!* Aethis assures himself, huffing.

"And? Don't give me any empty threats, Corsseussula, it's pointless and somehow makes you look even more idiotic. That giant man has no sense of how to kill me."

"Oh, yes, that is true."

She admits with a nod, her smile never wavering. It's as though she and Aethis had switched roles, and she was relishing the knowledge that she had him. She truly had him.

"Very true. But even if he can't kill you, he told me torturing you for all of eternity sounds just as promising."

Corsseussula lifts her long satin blue dress slightly, as if rearranging the silks calmly while the other stares at her in absolute mortification. Aethis has no chance, and he is well aware. He swallows hard, eyes flicking here and there rapidly. Corsseussula would never be this smug unless the time she was promising was near, which meant his time ran thin. He has very little time to do something. To try and save himself. He's a *god*, for the sake of mankind, and he had managed to get Corsseussula to bow to him! Why does he tremble at her threats?

She must be lying. Tricking him, to make him look even more like some kind of cheap fool.

He takes a breath and starts toward her, but that air is abruptly yanked from his lungs, and he is ripped off of his feet. He whirls around to see that a singular finger has been wrapped around his body, and he barely has time to think before the finger tightens around him, crushing his frame further.

Corsseussula doesn't even stay to watch the show play out, as she's seen the Creator's techniques, his skills, far too many times before to doubt him and what he can do. She turns abruptly, long flowing curls drifting down her back as she walks away from the scene, ignoring the shrieks and pleas of help from Aethis as the finger is joined by others, and then another hand, and he is pulled upward into the abyss of the sky, moments after he'd doubted her completely, after he'd given her such an entitled smirk, such an aura of smugness and overconfidence. She hums to herself as she speaks one message to Aethis before disappearing altogether, before letting Laphanae wreck him to pieces.

"You should really think twice before wronging my husband."

# The Aftermath II

Yureni opens his eyes. Yureni? His name? He almost jumps in shock. He is not nameless. Not anymore. Ah, yes!

He is elated. He can remember! Oh the joy! The joy lasts about a second.

The memories flood back to him, harshly sudden, cold and unforgiving, like a churning, icy river. His joy fades quickly and tears burn in his eyes.

*Oh no.*

*Oh God, no.*

He falls onto his knees. His body has no physical pain, no not one bit, but his mind is another story. Voices fill his head, bursting like explosives, making him cling onto his skull, as if afraid it will explode as well. The pain, the fear, the fury, the grief, the guilt…it all comes back to him in waves that slam into him, hammering him with agony. He feels as though his head is going to split open.

"Yureni."

The voice is sweet, like a comforting cool breeze on a warm summer night. At the sound, the pain fades away, and eventually disappears. Yureni is breathing heavily, still shaken and filled with remorse and misery, so much that he barely notices someone carefully kneel down in front of him. He looks up at them like a frightened fox. They gently caress Yureni's cheek, calming him, eyes wet with a smile on their face.

It's a young man with a bronze complexion and raven hair. Freckles cover his face, the back of his neck, and nearly everywhere else. Yureni remembers tracing them while explaining constellations, knowing the other didn't understand, but still smiling at him and nodding every time Yureni would get excited. His eyes are gray, like Yureni's own, but there's a twinge of brown near the edge.

Yureni's face crumples.

"Osuna?" he whispers, his voice breaking.

Osuna smiles wider, his copper eyes swimming with tears. Relief or regret? Yureni cannot tell.

"Yes. Yes, that's me," Osuna says, brushing away the tears threatening to spill. "It's me. I'm here."

Yureni bursts into sobs and embraces his lover tightly, as if letting go would split their fates again, leaving them separated forever, unable to apologize, unable to say farewell.

His nose turns pink while he sobs, a trait he'd had since he was a child. Better times.

"I'm sorry. I'm so, so sorry!" He cries, salty tears streaming down his cheeks as he bawls. He's never felt so vulnerable, so weak at his own lover's feet. But he feels as if he deserves every bit of that feeling and more, for his horrible actions.

"I never meant for you to get hurt, f-for anyone to get h-hurt…"

He sobs for a long time before his wails become small snivels and whimpers. Osuna strokes his hands, attempting to aid him in his misery.

"It's all right, Yureni. I know everything that happened now."

He speaks in a hushed voice, tone as light and gentle as the tides that brush up against a white, sandy shoreline.

"It wasn't your fault, my dear. It was not your fault."

Yureni sniffles pathetically. He doesn't believe him. No matter how many times he is told that he was not at fault for what he has done, he will never forgive himself.

"I just wanted us to be free. Free from that awful, awful place, that terrible life. I was willin' to do anythin' and everythin', Osuna. I was willin' to sacrifice everythin'," he says, voice so small it's almost silent, and it trembles like a small and watery earthquake.

There is a pause. Osuna pulls away from Yureni slightly. Before Yureni can protest, Osuna lightly kisses his forehead and sighs.

"Yureni, if only I'd known back then…" His eyes are shiny again. "Maybe I would've been able to save you."

They both are quiet for some time. Words don't have to pass between two people for them to understand each other. The silence is broken by a squeal, and both men lift their heads to glimpse the source.

A few meters away is a girl. She can't be older than seven, her face shows that much. She also has that sort of childish air about her. She is relatively small, olive skinned and freckled with bright gray eyes. Her blonde-white hair is in a long and partially messy braid down her back.

Yureni remembers that messy braid. Many times in the past, he had re-braided it when it came undone, which was quite often. Those moments of laughter when the braid would come undone, the memorization of those three pieces of hair and one specific pattern she always wore. He remembers those days of sunshine and peace, before everything.

"H-hemera?"

"Yureni!"

She runs over to them, embracing Yureni in a hug. Yureni is astounded. How a child could greet someone so cheerfully after all that person had done, to the child especially, was beyond him entirely. He slowly returns the hug with a faint smile.

He doesn't think he deserves the hug.

He doesn't even deserve to glance at her again.

He thinks this is too much, that he absolutely needs to apologize, needs to explain, needs to do something. He can't just not acknowledge the situation. He's caused too much suffering for them. And he needs to forgive himself and he needs them to forgive him.

Even though they probably won't. He still needs them to.

Hemera beams at him. She's a rather talkative child, Yureni remembers. The days she spent going on and on and on about the sky, the trees, even small things like a leaf. She once had a three hour long conversation about a specific freckle her brother had right below his eye.

The detail she'd gone into…. Yureni remembers this as happy, how she'd gone on about even the simplest things. For him, it had never been annoying at all. It had been interesting, and even fun. Walking down uncharted paths with her aboard his shoulders as they talked for hours about the trees and flowers they saw, or ones they'd hope to see.

He'd even been proud of her, for finding happy things to talk about even in the smallest of things in life. And just like she used to, now she doesn't waste a minute or a breath. The second she pulls away, it's like she is a wind-up toy someone has fully wound up. Her words tumble out like a river, too full.

"Brother and I waited so long for you! It felt like years! Has it been years? Time's fuzzy. How long has it been, Osuna? Five years? Ten?"

"Four hundred, Hemera."

"Oh! Yeah, four hundred years! Hehe, that's like for-ever. Four hundred years since we last saw you! Where have you been? The train's about to leave!"

Yureni chuckles quietly and brushes the back of his neck.

"Away. Away is all. I'm sorry I was gone for so long. Sorry I left you like that."

He hangs his head a bit with shame. The guilt still weighs him down, haunting him with every breath he takes, every heartbeat that resounds in his chest, every time he blinks…

He's made too many mistakes. Far too many. And horrible ones, no less.

What he's done is unforgivable, he knows. And he is well aware that any kind of forgiveness will not be something he will ever demand of them for this. How could they forgive him when he couldn't even forgive himself?

"I, um…I'm extremely sorry, Hemera. You as well, Osuna. I truly am. I never meant to hurt you, either of you, both of you. I love you both so very much, with my entire heart, and I can absolutely swear on everythin' I am, that I was never tryin' to hurt anyone. I know that sounds like a lie, or an excuse, and I assure you, it's not. I don't see a point in lyin' about this, but I-I wasn't myself when—"

"Eh."

Hemera waves him off as if he's apologizing for something stupid instead of literally apologizing for committing murder and cannibalism. Well, accidentally. Maybe that's why she's waving him off so nonchalantly. Or maybe it's for another reason? Yureni isn't sure, and he sort of doesn't want to know. He's surprised at this.

She gives him a half-smirk and plops down next to them both.

"Osuna already told me everything. About that stupid puppet guy and stuff. I know it wasn't really you, so don't apologize. I could kinda tell, anyway." She says with a shrug.

Children are finicky like that. They forgive easily, or they hold grudges and pout.

Hemera was the type of child to forgive easily, and Yureni was thankful for that. He isn't sure he forgives himself or believes her, even, but in that moment he is certainly content.

He knits his eyebrows together as he remembers a small but confusing detail Hemera had mentioned in her rambling. Didn't she mention something about a train?

"Hemera, what did you mean about a train?" He asks, genuinely puzzled. Hemera grabs his hand and starts to walk him in a direction ahead.

"The train to the afterlife, duh! The star train!"

Star train? Yureni looks up. And his breath is taken away.

It's like a train, but it's almost astral in a way. It is almost fully transparent, swirling with empty space and rays of sunlight, and memories, beliefs, wonders. It's beautiful. Faint clouds of white and light blue caress the side of this ethereal method of transportation. People already inside are laughing and content, the windows fogged with a slight bit of baby blue and white mist. The entire train is built like one would picture trains far before they were actually invented. It looks more elegant, albeit less complicated and intricate, and it had features that make it appear safer and more welcoming. It almost seems to glow, radiating a faint shine, inviting all to climb aboard.

Looking around, Yureni can see many other people, deceased souls like himself and his company, onboarding the train. Going to the afterlife? Must be. As he and his companions walk closer to it, Yureni is conflicted.

*Will he make it there?*

He had not always been the sweetest or bravest or most truthful in the first place.

The murders and cannibalism eliminated any bit of hope he had in passing on without guilt on his conscience. The worry etched onto his face catches the attention of Osuna, who touches his shoulder comfortingly.

"Yureni, it was not your soul that commanded you to do those things. Therefore, your soul will not be punished for those things, all right?"

Osuna's warm hand soothes his anxiety, and his words ease the strain on his mind. They always seemed to do that, but now more than ever.

Because, well, it was true.

Yureni had begged himself, his own body, to stop. And his own body had refused, instead following the command of someone Yureni couldn't even protect himself from. These facts made Yureni feel a great deal better. It was as if, for the first time, Yureni was actually not afraid or uncertain of the future. He was actually going to be okay.

Well, as okay as one can be with the cards he was dealt.

As soon as they come to the steps where they are to board this great machine of star and light, Hemera is buzzing with conversation again. Talking trees, birds, water, anything she can. Yureni can't blame her. Her brother does not respond to her ongoing chat that never seems to stutter, but he gives a faint smile. Two older people walk up to them. One with fiery red locks, the other with dark maroon.

Eventually, they both start to join in with the talking.

And the train departs, leaving only the faint sound of distant laughter. And Yureni joins in with the surrounding giggles.

For the first time in four hundred years.

# ABOUT THE AUTHOR

**C. McEntee** is a young author born in Massachusetts. She has been writing stories since she was seven, and can still distinctly remember her first grade teacher showing other teachers her work for a narrative exercise, which motivated her in her earlier years to continue writing.

In recent years, she became more interested in writing much longer stories (along with fanfiction, but nobody has to know about that), and testing out her writing abilities. Her first published work is *The Origins of A Star*, which she had started writing for fun while in 7th grade, and finished writing around her freshman year of high school.

The idea for this story sprang up from a dream she had about not being able to move on her own, and seeing her own body from outside, as a stranger. She plans on possibly making more books, though they will not be sequels to *The Origins of A Star*, and will have no connection to this book whatsoever. She plans on using any profits from her books to protect herself from "the pure, unbridled horror of college funds."

She thanks you greatly for reading.